‹ ‹ ‹

The Member-Guest

DOUBLEDAY

New York

London

Toronto

Sydney

Auckland

Clint
McCown

The
Member–
Guest

PUBLISHED BY DOUBLEDAY

a division of Bantam Doubleday Dell Publishing Group, Inc.

1540 Broadway, New York, New York 10036

DOUBLEDAY and the portrayal of an anchor with a
dolphin are trademarks of Doubleday, a division of Bantam Doubleday
Dell Publishing Group, Inc.

Library of Congress Cataloging-in-Publication Data

McCown, Clint, 1952–

The Member-Guest : a novel / Clint McCown. — 1st ed.

p.   cm.

1. Golf—Tournaments—United States—Fiction. 2. Suburban life—United
States—Fiction. 3. Country clubs—United States—Fiction.

I. Title.

PS3563.A2664M46   1995   94-28218

813'.54—dc20   CIP

ISBN 0-385-47655-8

March 1995

FIRST EDITION

1   3   5   7   9   10   8   6   4   2

Book design by Claire Naylon Vaccaro

in memory of
James E. McCown

and for
Cynthia

‹ ‹ ‹

Acknowledgments

"Music for Hard Times" was published in the *Sewanee Review* (volume 101, number 2, Spring 1993). Copyright 1993 by Clint McCown.

"Home Course Advantage" was published in *American Fiction* (number 2, 1991).

"Mule Collector" was published in *American Fiction* (number 4, 1993).

"Survivalists" was published in an altered form in *Northwest Review* (volume 22, numbers 2/3, 1984).

"Intermediate Swimming" was published in *Writers' Forum* (volume 19, 1993).

"Surface Tension" was published in the *Gettysburg Review* (volume 3, number 2, Spring 1990).

"Skull Shots" was published in *Denver Quarterly* (volume 27, number 2, Fall 1992).

"Design Flaws" was published in *Mid-American Review* (volume 13, number 2).

"Torch Song" was published in *Colorado Review* (volume 21, number 2, Fall 1994).

"Home Course Advantage" received the 1991 American Fiction Prize (judged by Louise Erdrich).

"Mule Collector" received the 1993 American Fiction Prize (judged by Wallace Stegner).

"Torch Song" was a finalist for the 1992 Nelson Algren Competition.

Thanks to these friends for their guidance: Dean Young, Scott Russell Sanders, Phil Appleman, David R. Young, David Milofsky, Emilie Jacobson, Scott Moyers, and Cynthia McCown; thanks also to the Wisconsin Arts Board and Beloit College for their support.

‹ ‹ ‹

The Member-Guest

‹ ‹ ‹

Home Course Advantage

Even while he was gluing the new set of grips on Mrs. Davies' old *Patty Berg* irons, Rod couldn't stop thinking about the carcass of the dog. The dewfall would have settled over it by now, which he hoped might dampen the smell. In the three days since he'd cut too sharply into the parking lot and caught the mangy stray unawares, the temperature had seldom dipped below ninety. This morning a couple of the club members had complained. The odor, they said, had been sucked in through their car air conditioners. They wanted it taken care of. The Member-Guest tournament was just a few days away, and a lot of out-of-towners would be coming in for practice rounds. It didn't speak well of the Club to leave a dead dog at the entrance to the parking lot.

So Rod had called the Highway Department to see if they'd come out and get the thing. They said they would, but it might take a couple of weeks—most of their trucks were tied up in the Route 15 bypass project, and roadkills had become a low priority. He told them he'd take care of it himself, and as he hung up the phone he made a mental note to pass the chore on to the Wickerham kid, who was running the grounds crew this summer.

But then the special shipment of Izods arrived, the one he'd ordered to beef up his sweater stock before the Member-Guest weekend, and he had to check the merchandise for damage. When he'd finally logged in all the stock numbers, he set to work assembling the eight-foot cardboard alligator they'd sent as a new promotional display. He was still trying to insert tab M into slot Q when Bev came in from the snack shop to tell him the freezer unit was making clacking noises and defrosting itself again. It took him half the afternoon to track down Ed Betzger, who held the service contract on all the Club's appliances, and by the time Ed had the unit working again, the ice-cream bars were showing clear signs of strain. So Rod had to call Teddy Mumford, the Club's insurance agent, to find out how far the meltdown had to go before the bars could be claimed as a loss. Here there was a point of contention. Teddy said a partial melting didn't constitute spoilage, and as long as the ice cream was uncontaminated it could still be sold. Rod explained that the bars didn't even look like bars anymore, but Teddy said the snack shop could feature them on the menu as a novelty item. Refrozen ice cream sounded exotic, Teddy told him, like refried beans. Rod said maybe it was time the Club got a new insurance agent.

Of course, that would never happen. Rod ran the day-to-day operations of the Club, but the Board of Directors made all the financial decisions; and Teddy Mumford was a member of the Board.

The injustice galled him, and as soon as he got off the phone with Mumford he stormed into the men's locker room to air a few complaints. But it was too late in the day, and there was no one there but Glen L. Hanshaw, himself one of the oldest Board members, sitting naked on the bench in front of his locker. It was a disconcerting sight, and Rod lost his momentum.

"Look at this crap!" Glen said, and he held up a pair of boxer shorts. "I haven't had these a goddamn month, and just look at them—the elastic's all shot to hell!" He threw them into the bottom of his locker and kicked the door closed with his foot. "I swear to Christ!"

Rod didn't know what to say, so he looked at his watch and hurried on down the row of lockers.

"Hey, wait a minute!" Glen pushed himself up from the bench and followed Rod to the side door. In the diffuse light of the windows, his skin took on a bluish pallor, like a body washed up from the sea. "I had a complaint about you today," he said. "Did I tell you?"

"What's the problem?"

"Shirley Davies says you were supposed to get her clubs back to her two weeks ago."

"The new grips haven't come in yet," he lied.

"Well, she was all over my ass about it." He ran a bony hand over his scalp. "I hear she's having a little trouble at home. Probably just needs to take it out on somebody. Anyway, I told her you'd take care of it. Right?"

Rod shrugged. "I'll see what I can do. If it's a holdup at the company, I know who to call. But if it's a problem with the shipping, we might have to reorder."

"Good man." Glen slapped him on the shoulder and padded off toward the showers. He moved unnaturally, Rod thought, as if he were picking his way across hot gravel. Strange what nakedness could do to some people. In his loud shirts and double-knit pants, Glen was the tyrant of his Cadillac dealership; here at the Club, all the kids who worked in the pro shop were afraid of him. But now he seemed just one more small animal caught outside its territory. Rod didn't know why, but the thought depressed him.

He climbed the stairs to his workroom and set about regripping Mrs. Davies' old irons. He got out the new grips and settled in on his bench by the window to start stripping the shafts. Only then did he remember that he'd never spoken to Jimmy Wickerham about getting rid of the dog. Now it was too late—the last few twilight stragglers were just coming in off the course. The grounds crew would have left hours ago. If Rod wanted the carcass disposed of before tomorrow, he'd have to do it himself.

It took him longer than usual to do the regripping. Somehow he mispositioned two of the new grips and had to strip both shafts and start again. The seven iron gave him particular trouble. The glue had hardened in a lump where the left thumb gripped the shaft, and though he knew Mrs. Davies would never know the difference, he couldn't let the imperfection pass. The seven iron was his favorite club, his luckiest club. He'd once holed out a hundred-and-seventy-yard approach shot with a seven iron on the final hole of the Doral Open. The eagle jumped him to eighth place, his best professional finish.

By the time he was satisfied with the positioning of all ten grips, it was after ten o'clock. He turned out the workshop light and stood for a minute by the window facing the highway. It was a moonless night, but the mercury-vapor lamp above the machine shed cast a yellow haze across the deserted parking lot. The dog lay just inside the edges of the light, and Rod could see clearly the dark lump waiting for him on the carpet of manicured grass.

But what exactly was he supposed to do with it?

He couldn't just sling it into the clubhouse Dumpster. The container wouldn't be emptied until next Tuesday morning, and six days of Dumpster heat was the last thing this dog needed.

He couldn't dump it anywhere on the course because the

grounds were so immaculately trimmed it was impossible to hide anything larger than a golf ball. The only exception was the bramble thicket that ran along the out-of-bounds to the left of the third hole, but that entire stretch was usually upwind from most of the course, and there was too much stink left in the animal to risk it.

He sure as hell wasn't about to load the remains into the back of his new Audi and go cruising around the countryside looking for a safe drop zone. He'd bought the car because he thought it might foster an image of stability and class—two things his ex-wife had often said he lacked—and he was certain that a lingering bad-meat smell would undercut his efforts. Besides, his trunk was full of all the unfinished paperwork he was supposed to be handling for the Club.

Of course, he could always take the Teddy Mumford approach of cheapskate practicality: run the carcass through the tree mulcher and spray the remains along the fairway for fertilizer. Even as he laughed at the thought, he felt a twinge of guilt. Mumford wasn't such a bad guy, really; he was just trying to keep the Club's premiums low. It had been a heavy year for claims against their current policy—there'd been some major plumbing and electrical problems, a fire in the women's locker room, vandalism on two of the greens, and a lot of theft. In the last two weeks alone they'd lost over eighteen thousand dollars' worth of equipment: three electric Cushman golf carts and a small tractor-mower. The insurance rates were bound to go up. Teddy had even told the

Board that unless the Club could find a way to hire a night watchman, the home office might not let him renew their policy at all.

Rod hoped they would hire a watchman. He also hoped they'd hire a Club manager, an accountant, a full-time assistant for the pro shop, and a couple of bag boys to help clean the members' clubs. Then maybe he'd have some time to work on his game. The way things stood now, he almost never got out on the course, and in the four years he'd been Club pro, he'd lost a lot of ground. His putting was pretty much the same as ever—it came in streaks, and he rarely missed anything under five feet. But he'd lost some of his touch on pitch-and-run shots, and even with his wedge he couldn't seem to make the ball bite the way it used to. His overall game was about four shots worse than when he'd started here. At that rate he'd be a duffer long before retirement age.

He knew it was his own fault. Nobody had forced him to take this job. In fact, he'd been happy to get it. The course had a good layout, and even though the Club ran on a pretty tight budget, enough money went into maintenance to keep it one of the finest nine-hole operations in the state. He didn't have to be ashamed of working here. Besides, he'd gotten tired of running with the rabbits, of driving from tournament to tournament all season long, scrambling for some share in the winnings. In three years he'd only made the cut nine times, and his career earnings wouldn't even cover his gas money. He quit the tour the week after the Doral Open, when his visibility was high enough to land him this steadier job. He didn't regret it. Even rookies had been finishing higher than Rod in the tournament standings, and the truth that sank into him after Doral was that eighth place was as high as he would ever go.

It was just as well, he told himself. He loved the game, but he wasn't cut out for business, and success made a business out of any game. Suppose he'd won the U.S. Open, or the Masters, or the PGA Championship: corporations would've come beating down his door for product endorsements. They'd have turned him into a "personality" and designed some ridiculous logo for his autographed line of leisurewear.

He did wonder what the logo might have been. Some animal, certainly—they were all animals. Alligators were already spoken for. So were penguins, seagulls, bears, jaguars, sharks, pandas, bulls, mustangs, dolphins, zebras, kangaroos, hawks, elephants, and flamingos.

No dogs, though—or at least none that he'd ever noticed. Certainly no dead stray dogs. No bloody, bashed-in half-breed German shepherds embroidered with infinite care into the tight weave of cotton-Orlon-Dacron-acrylic. If he ever did hit the big time maybe that could be his logo. He might even insist on it.

He picked up Mrs. Davies' seven iron to double-check the feel of it, and made his way downstairs and out the rear of the clubhouse. The night air was cool, and from the way the wind was gusting through the trees, he guessed a storm front might be moving in. Long rolls of heat lightning shimmered across the southern sky.

The window of the machine shed was unlocked, as usual, and Rod had no trouble reaching in for the shovel he knew would be hanging on the inside wall. As he walked across the lot toward the dead dog, a feeling of lightness came over him. Once he got the creature in the ground, the whole affair would be over. He'd never have to think about it again.

The night, he soon discovered, was the best possible time for the work. He'd been right about the smell: without the constant prodding of the sun, the flesh had sunk back into a more passive state of decay, and the dew seemed to keep the odor from rising. Only occasionally did little stabs of corruption dart up on the breeze, and by keeping the wind at his back and breathing carefully he was able to avoid most of the stench. The flies seemed to have settled down for the night —or maybe the wind was now keeping them at bay—and while there were probably slugs and other night workers swarming the rotten underside, they were all invisible, hidden by dog or darkness, so Rod could work easily, with his eyes open, in a way that would have been difficult for him in the full light of day.

The one thing that did bother him was the collar.

From the moment the animal had sprawled with a single yelp under the left front tire, Rod had avoided looking at it closely. He'd glimpsed enough to know the dog was a mixed breed, and from its general scruffiness he'd assumed it to be a stray. Now a queasy fear came over him that he'd open the morning paper and find some pathetic plea for the return of a family pet: Lost, in the vicinity of Route 30 west of town, a brown-and-black dog, part shepherd, answers to the name of . . .

A silver tag gleamed in the pale light. On it, Rod knew, there would be some identification, but he couldn't bring himself to bend his face down close enough to read what the inscription might say. Instead, he carefully hooked the head of Mrs. Davies' seven iron underneath the collar and began to drag the dead dog toward the putting green. The body stayed perfectly curled, firm now as a piece of sculpture as it scraped along the gravel lot. The weight of the thing surprised him. Until now he'd thought of the carcass as just a husk, and it amazed him to realize that the dog was no less substantial for the fact of having died.

He circled below the putting green and drew the dog alongside the practice bunker. The raised lip between the bunker and the green spread a less diluted night across the sand so that at first the trap seemed bottomless, a sinkhole yawning in the grassy slope. But soon his eyes adjusted, and the shadow gave way to the dingy sparkle of the sand itself. It was a perfect spot. The digging would be easy here, and when he was through there would be no broken turf to give the grave away.

He stepped down into the bunker and began shoveling

the whiter top sand into a far corner to keep it separate from the brown foundation grit and the reddish dirt that lay below. It took him only six or seven minutes to work his way down through the natural layer of topsoil, and though his progress then slowed from the increasing density and rockiness of the ground, he continued to make headway.

It felt good to work the shovel in the earth, so good he started humming as he dug, improvising variations on a single jazzy theme for nearly half an hour, until suddenly, as he strained to pry loose a stubborn, buried stone, it came to him what song it was, and with that thought the sound of it died away in his throat. It was a song that had haunted him for weeks now.

He didn't even know its name, but he took it to be an old blues number, maybe from the Billie Holiday era. The lyrics were hazy to him—some usual fare about love gone wrong —but what still burned in his mind was the one time he'd heard it, sitting in Herr's tavern drinking his fourth double scotch, alone at a corner table in the otherwise crowded bar. A woman, heavily made-up but still somehow breathtaking, swayed on a low platform by the far wall and sang, with her eyes closed, in the voice of a grieving angel. Even through the smoke and the room's dim amber glow, he could see that her hair was red, deep red, and it clung in damp curls to her cheek and forehead. Her pale skin seemed unearthly, perfect, fragile as glass. Rod could have believed she was all the beauty left in the world; and that she was dying, now, in front of him. He envied her the grandeur of such public despair.

When her song was over, she opened her dry eyes and smiled warmly at the crowd, nodding to specific groups for their whistles and applause. Then her whole face brightened —she'd spotted someone at Rod's end of the room—and without hesitation she climbed down from the makeshift stage, her bent leg spilling through the slit in her gown. She wove her way between the tables toward him, and he watched her intently as she moved, fascinated by the ease with which she'd left the song behind, like a snake shedding skin, or a butterfly, maybe, abandoning an outworn cocoon. It wasn't until she reached his chair that he realized he was the person she was crossing to meet, and before he could offer up any question she flung an arm around his neck and kissed him earnestly on the mouth. He was as stunned as if he'd been hit by a truck.

As she drew her face away from his, he opened his mouth to fumble toward some trite compliment about her singing, but before he could manage even a syllable a dark change came into her eyes, and she pulled herself up straight.

"My God," she said, her right hand fluttering to her cleavage. "You're not Randy!" A bubble of embarrassed laughter broke from her throat, then she turned abruptly toward the stage. "Hey, Marcie," she called, "look at this guy!" Half the heads in the room turned in Rod's direction. "Doesn't he look just like Randy?"

A woman from a table near the bar seemed to struggle for a moment with the task of bringing Rod into focus, then sank back into a confused frown. "You mean that's not him?"

"Hell, no! Can you believe this? And Christ, I just gave him a big wet one." Several people laughed, and she turned again to Rod. "Sorry, sugar. Thought you were somebody else." She patted him on the cheek and threaded her way casually to the bar.

Rod felt like she took his whole identity with her. It was as if, for a few accidental seconds, he'd seen himself through her eyes and found that he was utterly invisible, a man so bland he could enter a look-alike contest for himself and still come away the loser. A shudder ran through him, and a spinning rose in his head that nearly tipped him over. He left the tavern without finishing his drink.

By now he'd achieved a pit nearly three feet deep, which he judged sufficient. He tossed the shovel into the hole and sat heavily on the upper rim of the trap. He was more than winded: the work had turned nasty toward the end and now ropes of undeveloped muscle began to knot along his back. He probably wouldn't be able to swing a club for a week. Still, he felt a sense of accomplishment, and in his sudden stupor of exhaustion he felt less finicky toward the condition of the dog—though he resisted the impulse to pat its mangled head.

The wind was stronger now and felt good against the side

of his face, but the change in weather worried him. Clouds were swirling in thick and low, and if he didn't get the dog belowground in a hurry, he might end up soaked when the bottom dropped out. He pushed himself up from the bank and grabbed Mrs. Davies' seven iron, which was still hooked under the collar. The dog slid easily down the slope to the edge of the grave.

"Roll over!" Rod said, and with a twist of the iron the carcass disappeared into the hole. "Now, stay!" With some difficulty he retrieved the club, then tamped down the body with the shovel. The snug fit pleased him, though he felt somehow disconcerted that in the underground darkness he couldn't tell whether the dog had landed on its back or on its stomach. He even thought about getting a flashlight from the clubhouse to find out, but in the end fatigue convinced him to let it go. The dog wouldn't care, so why should he?

He was just pouring in the first shovelful of dirt when a pair of headlights swept across him from the highway. He froze like a startled animal and watched a large flatbed truck wheel into the lot. It pulled up by the machine shed fifty yards away, and a burly man in overalls climbed down from the cab. Rod saw at once that the man was ill at ease. Body movement, after all, was his specialty: he knew how to read imperfections in a stance, a turn, a swivel, a follow-through; and he watched this trespasser now with a coldly professional eye.

Whatever the guy was up to, it seemed to Rod that he

needed lessons. There was a tightness in the man's shoulders, and he moved his head with a birdlike jerkiness as he scanned the dark outer reaches of the lot. Rod knew he was too far away to be seen, particularly by anyone standing so near the security light, so he kept still and let the blind stare pass through him. There was something appealing in this—in seeing without being seen, as if he were no more than a ghost—but the interest Rod had in that aspect of the situation was offset by the column of stench now rising from the pit at his feet. He set the shovel down gently in the sand and eased his way upwind to the cleaner, whiter corner of the trap. He was just crouching below the smooth cut of the lip when the man in the lot let out a loud, shrill whistle. Rod thought at first he'd been spotted, but then he realized that the man wasn't looking his way. He was turned toward the machine shed with his head cocked to the side as if he were listening for something.

Rod listened, too. Except for the wind rustling the trees, everything was quiet. Even the crickets and frogs from the drainage ditch behind the first tee had grown still under the expectation of rain.

Then the man whistled again, but instead of waiting for a response he reached in through the window of the truck and took out what appeared to be a small tackle box. The next few steps were all too predictable. After so many years of golf, Rod knew how to trace a trajectory, and had only to watch the swing to know where the ball would land. When the man walked to the rear window of the machine shed and climbed inside, Rod could only shake his head. God, how he hated amateurs.

He climbed out of the trap and walked across the parking lot to the truck, Mrs. Davies' seven iron in hand. For a moment he considered bashing in the windshield, but gestures like that were more dramatic than effective; and anyway it might hurt the club. Instead, he just took the keys from the ignition and walked calmly back to his bunker. It was a good first move, he told himself. Every match hinged on psyching out the opponent.

A minute later the front door of the shed swung open and one of the new Cushman gas-powered carts came nosing silently out. Apparently the man had been unable to hotwire it, in spite of his tool kit, and he now trotted alongside the cart, pushing and steering at the same time. He maneuvered the Cushman into position behind the truck, then pulled out a pair of long planks from the flatbed and propped them in place as a ramp. After lining up the steering for a straight shot at the boards, he got behind the cart and heaved it forward. Rod thought this a foolish technique—the wheels could easily miss one of the rails or skid over the side halfway up to the truck. But the man seemed unconcerned, and when the front left wheel did slip from its plank, he was able to hold the four-hundred-pound cart level as he walked it forward into the bed of the truck. Rod was glad he hadn't smashed this guy's windshield.

As he watched the thief slide the planks back onto the truck, Rod wondered why he hadn't just slipped into the clubhouse and called the police. What made him think he had to handle this himself? He'd always been a smart money player, always staying with the high-percentage shot; and he knew better than to try to clear a hazard when the odds told him to play up short. Still, it was too late to worry about it now. The time to think was before the shot; never in mid-swing.

He took a golf ball from his pocket and dropped it into the spongy grass just off the apron of the practice green. Then he took a narrow stance almost directly behind the ball and opened the face of the seven iron. It was a trick he'd learned for putting more loft into a club, and though he'd never used the shot in competition because it was too difficult to control, he'd always known it was there if he needed it. He took a full swing across the ball, playing it more or less like a bunker shot, and with a sharp *click!* it vanished upward into the night.

The man across the lot was just lashing the cart to the flatbed when the clean sound of contact froze him in place, still as a photograph. For a full five seconds he held his pose, listening into the darkness. Then with a loud metallic *thunk,* the ball came down on the hood of the truck. It broke the stillness like a starter's gun, and the man bounded into the cab of the truck, slamming the door behind him.

Rod walked forward into the light and crossed the parking lot in long, brisk strides, like a tournament leader approaching the eighteenth green. He paused by the rear of the truck and for a long moment the two men stared at each other's reflections in the side-view mirror. At last the door swung open, and the cart thief climbed slowly out.

He was bigger than he'd seemed from across the lot— maybe six foot five—and old enough that middle age had parceled his bulk evenly between muscle and flab. His face was round, almost childlike, with a dark, sparse beard that sprouted in random patches over his cheeks. As he faced Rod in the gravel, he tucked his hands in his overalls with an air of defiant calm. His mouth hung slightly open, and his dull eyes looked haggard even in the dim light. Rod felt certain the man was not a golfer.

"Evening," he said. The man nodded and coughed, but didn't speak. "I notice you've got one of our carts here."

The man glanced briefly to the cart, then took a studied look around him, as if he'd only that moment realized where he was. "Yeah, well, we got a call to pick it up for some repairs. The transmission's gone bad."

"You work odd hours."

The man shrugged. "Some days are like that."

Rod reached up and touched the fiberglass body of the new cart. "You know, I hate these bastards. They're an insult to the game."

"That so?" the man asked, nudging the gravel with the toe of his work boot.

"Yeah. They kill the grass. Most of the really good courses don't even allow them on the grounds." He shook his head at the cart, which gleamed in the glow of the vapor lamp. "But we're not exactly the Augusta National here, so I've got to put up with them. I even have to fix them when they break down. So I know you didn't get a call from anybody."

The man's slack-jawed pose fused into a more natural scowl. "Then you must have my keys," he said, and started toward Rod, who shifted into a bunker stance and drew the seven iron to the top of his backswing.

"Buddy, I know how to use a golf club," he said. It was one of the few positive statements he could make about his life, and he was amazed at how little impact it had. The man hesitated for a moment—only for a moment—then, with his eyes fixed on the thin shaft of the iron, he gave a skeptical snort and lumbered into range.

The swing Rod used was smooth and relaxed—so much so that even the cart thief himself might have thought it was a halfhearted effort. But the timing was there, and that's where the power lay in golf. There was a trick to it, like ringing the bell with a sledgehammer at the county fair. Rod rang the bell now. With a good body turn and a snap of his wrists, he transferred the entire momentum of his arc into the club face. This was no stubby punch shot for getting out of tree trouble, but a full swing and follow-through, the kind that cuts down hard behind the ball and takes a deep, long divot. It did so now: the heavy blade caught the lower edge of the man's right kneecap and moved on through the shot for a clean, high finish.

With a startled gulp, the man tottered slowly sideways and crumpled to the rough pavement, too stunned at first to utter a sound. But that moment passed, and he launched into a shrill whine as he squirmed frantically on his crippled leg.

Rod stepped back to gauge the damage: the club was okay; the guy would be on crutches for a while. "I'm really sorry about this," he said.

The man glared up at him and spoke through clenched teeth. "I oughta kill you, you son of a bitch!" He looked as if he had more to say, but a fresh pain twisted through his leg and kept any words from forming. He turned his face away with a groan and began to rock back and forth in the gravel.

"I could call a doctor," Rod offered, but the man ignored him. He rolled onto his left side and whistled once more like he had when he'd first climbed down from the truck. The effort hurt him, and he groaned again. A queasiness rose up from the pit of Rod's stomach. "What are you whistling for?" he asked, though he thought he knew.

A strained smile broke across the man's face. "Somebody to tear your goddamn arm off," he said, and fell into a giddy laugh.

"It's a dog, isn't it?" Rod asked.

"It's a bitch," the man answered, and began to giggle

uncontrollably. He leaned his weight back on his elbows and tried to straighten his leg in front of him, but the knee wouldn't unbend. "Christ," he said, still giggling, "what the hell have you done to me?"

"I think you've gone into shock," Rod told him.

The man lowered his head to the gravel and lay as still as he could through the small spasms of laughter, taking slow, deep breaths until he finally brought the pain under control. At last he raised himself up and leaned heavily against the grimy rear wheel.

"What about the dog?" Rod asked.

The man sighed and stared down at his crooked leg. "She got away from me last week," he said.

"What the hell do you mean she got away from you?" The sharpness in Rod's tone surprised them both.

"I mean she jumped out of the truck to run down a rabbit," the man said, now keeping a wary eye on Rod's seven iron. "I couldn't wait around."

Rod hacked the club hard into the pavement, sending up sparks and a small spray of stones. The man flinched and huddled closer to the wheel.

"You asshole," Rod shouted. "Don't you know better than to leave a dog to run loose by a highway?"

The man shrugged. "I came back," he said.

Rod hated simple answers. They weren't enough. Besides, they always seemed to back him into corners. For as long as he'd been a part of the game, he could remember only two times when he'd given in to simple answers, and both times he'd felt cheated.

The first was when he was a boy, playing with his father's clubs. His father had been a left-hander, so for his first two years in the sport, Rod had been a left-hander, too. Then when he was twelve his father bought him a right-handed set. He was furious about having to start learning all over again, and he demanded a reason for his father's forcing him to give up so much ground. "You're not left-handed," his father told him.

The second time was when he decided to quit the tour.

He felt the same frustrations building up in him now, as if he were still somehow playing on the wrong side of the ball.

"You can keep the cart," he said.

The man narrowed his eyes. "What?"

"I said you can keep the cart. We've got insurance."

The man slowly pulled himself up on his good leg and steadied his weight against the side of the flatbed. "That doesn't sound right. What's the catch?"

"I want you to give me your dog."

"What?"

"I want your dog."

The man looked around uneasily. "I told you, I already lost her."

"Then there shouldn't be any problem. From now on we can just say she belongs to me."

"And that's it?"

"That's all."

The man chewed on the inside of his cheek for a moment, and nodded. "Yeah, okay. Sure." Then he frowned. "What about my keys?"

Rod pointed to the darkness at the lower end of the lot. "There's a sand bunker just below that ridge," he said. "You might start looking down there."

The man eyed him suspiciously. "How am I supposed to do that? I can't even walk."

Rod extended the club head toward him. "You can have this."

The man reached carefully forward and took the iron from Rod's hand. "Okay," he said, then shifted his weight onto the shaft of the club and limped away from the truck. He circled wide around Rod and made his way cautiously toward the edge of the dark. Rod watched him until he'd reached the bunker, then took the keys from his pocket and tossed them through the open window of the cab.

He'd have to order Mrs. Davies a new seven iron. She'd be mad as hell when he told her he'd lost this one. She'd probably try to get him fired. But that was okay. Sometimes you just had to give up what you were used to, or you might never get anything right.

For now, though, the only thing he wanted to think about was hitting a bucket of range balls. He'd lost a little control lately, he knew that; and if he didn't work on it, his problems would only multiply. Golf was an unforgiving game, with no use for shortcuts or excuses. A good swing was built on fundamentals. The grip, the stance, the take-away, the body turn, the follow-through—all had to be kept in balance. If one went wrong, the rest collapsed like a house of cards.

He would start with his wedge to see how his short game was holding up. Then he'd work his way right up through the driver.

But he'd have to hurry. The wind was rising stronger now, and it swept in from the course with the clean smell of the coming storm. To the south he could see the glow of the town lights against the low-hanging clouds. The rain hadn't hit quite yet, but it would before long.

He knew it was bound to.

Intermediate Swimming

When she was through scraping the grease from the grill and changing the oil in the fry vat, Bev settled herself on one of the counter stools and stared toward the takeout window, waiting. A pair of flies had tormented her all morning, and since the two-day string of thunderstorms had robbed her of her customers, there had been little else to hold her attention beyond the annoying buzz. She'd nailed the slow fat one early in the afternoon on the spout of the Pepsi dispenser, but the other was quick and smart and never seemed to land in the open. She knew sooner or later it would head for the window and bump in confusion against the rain-streaked glass. In that moment of disorientation she would make her move with the swatter. Then a quick squirt of Windex, a

pass with a paper towel, and she'd be finished: the snack bar would be ready for tomorrow's practice round of the Member-Guest tournament.

She'd looked at the sign-up sheet in the pro shop—over two hundred golfers had already paid their registration fees. If the rain didn't kill it all, this would be her biggest weekend of the year. The Club had more than its share of cheapskates, but whenever a tournament rolled around they all wanted to look like big spenders. Cheesy salesmen who normally would've schemed to get her last nickel in a car deal would stuff ten-dollar bills into her tips glass even if all she did was hand them a beer. Bank presidents and airline pilots would camp out on her barstools to brag about their good shots or whine about their bad, and if she feigned an interest they'd leave a twenty on the counter to cover a two-dollar tab. Some of the divorced lawyers might try to flirt with her—though that side of her life was slowing down now that she was pushing forty—and if she smiled back at the right moment, or let some sunburned insurance agent touch her arm as she passed him a plate of fries, who knew how much she might rake in?

She'd have to watch herself, though. Her flirtations sometimes got a little out of hand. How else could she explain Ed Betzger? Ed hadn't appealed to her at all, not really—he smoked cigars, he rarely shaved, he never said anything that struck her as even remotely interesting, and, as near as she could tell, his whole wardrobe consisted of an alternating pair of white electrician's overalls, neither of which seemed to fit him very well. When he'd first come around last month to install the snack bar's new freezer unit, she'd barely noticed him. But then he kept showing up—sometimes on service calls, since he was the contractor on all the Club's heating and cooling systems, and sometimes just to eat a burger and shoot the breeze. He talked a lot about freon emissions and BTUs, which at first made her peg him as a pretty sad case. But after a while she began to enjoy his company, dull as it was. She had always felt sort of weedlike at the Country Club, so it was nice to have someone else around who seemed equally out of place. She kidded around with him a few weeks before anything really happened, but when it did she surprised herself by thinking: Yeah, sure, why not?

She'd been married to Stan only five months at the time.

The freezer unit shut itself off, ending the electric hum she had until that moment failed to notice. She listened for other sounds, but there weren't any. The rain had kept even the regulars away, and except for Rod, who had to run the pro shop at the other end of the building, the clubhouse was deserted.

Then came the soft erratic buzz of the fly bumping against the windowpane. Bev slid from her stool and crept alongside the counter, swatter in hand. The buzzing grew louder as she neared the window, but still she didn't see the fly anywhere among the water beads and rivulets. When she drew close enough to study the entire pane, she realized the fly was not there. Then the buzzing stopped. She held her pose and waited.

Maybe the buzz had come from somewhere else, she thought. The hearing in her left ear was sharp, but the right had suffered nerve damage from an infection when she was a girl—not enough to make her hard of hearing, but enough to distort her placement of sound. That never bothered her, really, except when she was alone at night. Then every slammed car door, every barking dog, every sudden shift of wind sounded wrong to her, like warnings crowding in from all directions. Stan, of course, had been the solution to that problem. His ears were fine. He always knew where every sound was coming from.

As she stood before the window, listening for the fly and staring blindly at the rain blurring the glass, her eyes suddenly focused on the swimming pool outside. The pool had been closed for two days because of the storms, but now the gate on the chain-link fence stood wide open and something broad and dark floated in the deep end. Bev's first thought was that it was a black inner tube left behind by one of the kids, but when she stepped closer to the window and peered between two long streaks of rain, she realized what it really was. Someone—a woman, it looked like, from her swimsuit —was floating face-down in the water.

Bev's mind leapt backward to an old, old drill, and suddenly, without thought or plan, a layer of her life was stripped away. An energy she hadn't known she still possessed sprang up in her, and quick as that, like the throwing of a switch, the snack bar simply vanished, and she became again the lifeguard at Rehoboth Beach, reacting as she'd been trained, with speed and strength and hardened self-control.

But Rehoboth Beach was twenty years past, and as Bev burst through the lounge door onto the wet sidewalk, her body lagged behind the sprint her mind had set. How long had it been since she'd run anywhere? The muscle along the back of her right thigh cramped instantly and she pitched forward onto the concrete, still twenty yards from the edge of the pool.

"Shit!" she screamed, and pulled herself up by the gatepost. Her thigh was on fire, but she knew a leg cramp wouldn't drown her, not in a swimming pool where there wasn't much distance to cover. She could still manage, surely. Besides, movement might come easier once she got in the water. She let go of the gate and limped as quickly as she could toward the woman's bobbing form, all the while rehearsing the procedure in her mind. The cramp would keep her from taking off her shoes, which complicated things, but everything else could be done by the book—what she remembered of it. Luckily the woman's feet were extended toward her, so Bev could come at her from behind and underneath, as she was supposed to. She only hoped the woman wouldn't struggle when she got jerked under for the cross-chest hold. That was always a moment of panic for anyone still conscious, and a panicked drowner could drag down even the strongest swimmer. But that shouldn't be a problem here—this woman seemed pretty far gone. Bev thought she spotted some slight movement in the arms, but on the whole the woman was already in the passive stage. That meant there wasn't any time to waste, but it also meant the rescue should be easy, which was a relief. With her right leg knotted by the cramp, Bev knew she couldn't handle much resistance.

She lunged headlong into the pool and struggled her way toward the bottom. The water felt warm compared to the rain, and when she peered up through the chlorine to gain her bearings, she could see the woman above her with surprising clarity. She was large, and in her black one-piece suit she seemed to float above Bev like an island. Her hair was black, too, and it fanned straight out from her head in a dark aura. She wore white goggles and her mouth hung open, giving her face a frozen, startled look. Each of the woman's legs seemed enormous, and Bev felt grateful for what she'd learned in her old lifesaving class: "No one is fat in the water," the instructor had told them. He was a big man himself—a bulky ex-jarhead named Gus she'd had a crush on at the time—and he always made them practice their rescues on him instead of each other because he could put up the most desperate fight. "Don't ever expect cooperation," he used to tell them. "You can't save a life without taking a prisoner."

Bev reached up, grabbed the woman's ankles, and jerked downward as hard as she could, at the same time climbing up along the broad body to hook her arm across the woman's neck and chest. The move took only a second, but the response was immediate: the woman began to thrash about wildly, kicking her feet and twisting awkwardly from side to side in a frantic attempt to shake Bev from her back. It was basically the same move Gus used to spring on her, and now, even with the handicap of her useless leg, Bev was ready for it. She clamped her forearm in place and held on tight, knowing she could ride the woman's panic all the way to a blackout if she had to.

But this woman seemed bigger even than Gus, and the strength wouldn't go out of her. She spun ferociously, clawing her way in circles through the water. Bev tried to force the two of them toward the surface, but without the kick of her right leg she couldn't make any headway. They hung there for a long moment, a tangle of two bodies suspended helplessly above the drain, until finally, with no forewarning at all, the woman simply stopped struggling and let her arms sink to her sides. In the sudden calm Bev could feel the ragged pounding of a heart, though she couldn't tell whose. She shifted her arm to get a better grip, and knew at once she shouldn't have. The woman jabbed a massive elbow into

Bev's rib cage, and the blow knocked her breath out in a spew of bubbles.

She had no choice now but to surface. She released her hold, planted her left foot in the center of the woman's back, and shoved clear. The woman was still flailing as Bev turned and kicked her way clumsily toward the side of the pool.

She surfaced within reach of the ladder, and clung to it for a few quick gulps of air. The knot in her thigh clenched tighter now, more crippling than before, and she knew she'd have to relax it somehow before going under again. She closed her eyes and tried to take a long, steady breath, but the churning water lapped against the pool wall and washed backward into her face, burning her nose and throat with chlorine. She began to cough so violently she thought her lungs would collapse. Her whole body seemed to have mutinied, and as she stood there on the ladder's bottom rung, choking up what she'd swallowed and fighting not to feel the pain now devouring her leg, despair took hold and told her what she dreaded most: she couldn't help the woman in the pool. Not now, at least, not until she'd regained some control—and that might be too late. She pressed her head against the aluminum rail, bracing for the sobs now building in her chest. The rain felt cold on her shoulders, even through her shirt. She stared down into the water at the madras sleeve billowing around her arm. The darkest colors drifted from the cloth in cloudy trails.

Then from behind her came the splashing and the screams.

The woman had surfaced on the far side of the pool, and even amid her choke and sputter for new breath, she was shrieking. Bev turned in the water to see, and as the woman heaved herself against the safety of the pool wall, propping her arms at last along the concrete deck, Bev's tension and her sharpest pains all fell away in gratitude. If it weren't for the water still singeing the tops of her lungs, she might have cheered.

But the woman kept screaming. She tried once to pull herself out onto the deck, but she couldn't get more than her waist past the waterline. She sank slowly down again.

Bev tried to speak, but managed only another coughing fit. The woman looked back over her shoulder. "Don't you come near me!" she yelled.

"It's okay," Bev called hoarsely. "Just relax. You're all right now."

"Relax?" she screamed, ripping the goggles from her face. "You tried to kill me!"

It was Shirley Davies. She and her husband, Lyle, had been Club members for about two years. He was a nice enough guy—a real estate agent who left dollar tips even if he only bought a candy bar—but she was harder to please. Earlier in the summer she had tried to make Rod fire one of the pro-shop kids for stealing three clubs from her bag. It turned out she'd left them in a sand trap on the fifth hole, but that didn't soften her attitude: she still complained to the Board about Rod because he hadn't taken her seriously. He ended up having to give her a dozen free golf lessons to smooth things over.

Bev's own experience with Mrs. Davies had been limited to the everyday commerce of the snack bar, and nothing out of the ordinary had ever passed between them. She sometimes felt Mrs. Davies gave her hard looks, as if something were wrong—but since she couldn't think of any reason for it, Bev had decided it was just her imagination. Still, she kept a tight smile on her face whenever Mrs. Davies came in for lunch, and she served extra fries with the hamburgers.

"I was saving you," Bev said. She hooked her left arm around the top rung of the ladder and reached down with the other to massage the cramp from her leg.

Mrs. Davies slashed the water with the side of her arm, sending a wall of spray toward Bev that vanished into the rain-pocked surface between them. "Goddammit, you almost drowned me!"

"I was saving you," Bev said again, calmly as she could. In her two summers at Rehoboth Beach, she'd never actually had to rescue anyone, but she'd heard enough stories from other lifeguards to know that Mrs. Davies would naturally be disoriented at first.

"I didn't need saving! I was fine!"

"You weren't fine," Bev told her. She tried to keep her

voice smooth and comforting, but the words stiffened in her throat and came out strained, as if she were lecturing an unruly child. "You were in trouble."

"I was not!" Mrs. Davies lowered her chin to her breast and shuddered. Then she snapped her head up sharply and glared across the water at Bev. "How could you be so stupid!"

Bev felt the prickle of blood rising to her face. "Look, I know you're confused right now. That's understandable. But you were floating face-down in the water."

Mrs. Davies waved her goggles viciously at Bev. "Of course I was face-down in the water! I was looking for something on the bottom!"

It was clearly true. Bev's insides fell away like cinder blocks, leaving a numbed, hollow cavity behind. Rehoboth Beach receded, and the world of the snack bar settled its familiar weight across her shoulders. "But the pool's closed!" she managed to say at last. "What the hell were you looking for?"

Mrs. Davies scowled down at the water for a long moment, then carefully slipped the goggles back over her head. "None of your damned business."

Bev gripped the sides of the ladder and pulled herself out of the pool. "Fine," she said, wringing her shirttail onto the wet concrete. "But you'll have to get out now. Like I said, the pool's closed." She tugged her soaked blue jeans higher on her hips, then crossed her arms and stared down at Mrs.

Davies, waiting for her to cross the pool and climb out. But Mrs. Davies didn't budge.

"You don't even know who I am, do you?" she said.

"Sure, I know who you are. You're Shirley Davies." A sharp roll of thunder passed overhead, and Bev nodded toward the sky. "But there's lightning up there that wouldn't know you from Adam, so I suggest you get your butt out of the water right now."

Mrs. Davies stared at her without making a move. "I'm not Shirley Davies," she said, but she spoke so softly Bev wasn't sure she'd heard her right. Then Mrs. Davies fastened her with a hard look, the same look Bev remembered from the snack bar. "You really don't know me, do you?"

Bev held her stance, but she began to feel uncomfortable, as if her brittle attitude, which had been perfectly appropriate only a moment before, were now completely out of place. She shifted her weight to her sore leg, then immediately thought better of it and shifted back again. Water squished noisily through the toes of her sneakers.

"I don't know what you're talking about," she said.

"I'm Shirley Stonesifer. Before I got married I was Shirley Stonesifer. I was a year behind you in high school."

Bev frowned down at the woman in the pool. The name meant nothing to her.

"We had a study hall together one year," she continued. "And you used to date my cousin, Ricky Staub."

God, Ricky Staub. Bev hadn't thought about him in years. She'd gone out with him a few times the summer her mother died. He'd even gone with her once to the hospital. She remembered standing with him at the end of a corridor outside her mother's room, looking out the window. That was the only time in her life she'd ever seen—actually seen—the wind. They were eight floors up, and below them was a sloping hillside of tall grass. The grass swayed with each turn of the breeze, charting a trail of pure motion as the wind rippled and curled and leapt across the field, sometimes splitting into separate channels, then reuniting into tiny whirlwinds that gently spun themselves out. The summer air seemed liquid to her then, a flow of intricate and vanishing designs, a writing she could never quite decipher. That one moment outside her mother's room was all she remembered now about being with Ricky Staub, though she knew they'd gone to a few movies and dances together. He was a cute boy, but things just hadn't worked out between them. She couldn't remember why.

Shirley Stonesifer pushed away from the side and paddled gracelessly across the pool. Her stroke seemed faltering, at best, and by the time she reached the ladder she was breathing heavily. She drew herself in against the top rung and looked up at Bev. "I was a lot thinner back then. I was never a hot ticket like you, but I looked all right."

Bev didn't like hearing herself described as a hot ticket,

but she let it pass. She had probably scared this woman half to death; the least she could do now was show a little kindness. "I think I remember you," she lied. "Didn't you have a nickname or something?"

"No. Just Shirley."

Bev uncrossed her arms and shivered in the wind. Streaks of purple dye ran from her cuffs across the backs of her hands. "Well, how's Ricky doing these days?"

Shirley eased away from the ladder and began to tread water. "He died about ten years ago."

Bev opened her mouth to speak, but could think of nothing reasonable to say. The news unnerved her—not because she'd ever felt much for Ricky, but simply because ten years had passed without her knowing he was dead. A full decade: the news was now so cold and distant it could pass for history, so weightless to the world that even Ricky's cousin could shrug it off as coolly as a change in weather. How could she have let herself drift so far out of touch?

"It was all pretty dumb-assed," Shirley went on. "He drank two quarts of gin on a dare."

"That stuff'll kill you," Bev said, stupidly.

Shirley watched her for a moment, then shook her head. "Anything'll kill anybody," she said, then rolled onto her stomach and breaststroked toward the shallow end. She stopped at the divider rope to catch her breath.

"Look," Bev said, "you really have to get out now. I've got to get back to the snack bar."

"Not in those clothes," Shirley said. "You'll drip chlorine all over the lounge carpet."

"Well, then I'll have to go home and change. But I can't do anything until you get out the pool."

"Why not?"

"I'm responsible. When the pool's closed, I'm supposed to keep people out."

"Hey, don't sweat it." Shirley smiled and began to bob on her toes in the shallower water. "I know how to swim. And the lightning's too far away to worry about."

"I don't care, I'm still responsible."

"You didn't used to be." She held her smile, but there was no friendliness in it, and for a fleeting second Bev really did seem to remember the younger version of this woman— a snide harpy who used to hang around the fringes of Bev's group making wisecracks. But maybe not.

"What's that supposed to mean?" she asked.

"In high school. You were pretty wild back then. You always seemed to do whatever you wanted."

The rain had nearly stopped, but a cold gust broke across Bev's back and she shivered again. "Nobody does what they want in high school."

Shirley stopped bobbing. "Maybe not," she said. She pushed the thick nylon cord underwater and balanced herself on it like a tightrope walker. "Anyway, high school's over. We're grown-ups now. We can all do anything we want. I mean, wasn't that supposed to be the deal?"

Bev rubbed the goose bumps along the backs of her arms. "I need to go," she said. "I was about to lock up for the day. I've got to pick my husband up from the hospital by five."

Bev regretted at once that she'd mentioned Stan. Shirley stopped moving in the water and tilted her head slightly, as if she were listening to a piece of music that had just changed key.

"Is that where he works?" she asked.

Bev hated questions about her private life, but Shirley had too many claims on her now to get brushed off. "He's a patient," she said. "He had to go in for a knee operation. He got hurt on the job a couple of nights ago."

Shirley stepped off the rope and let it ride up between her legs. "Sorry to hear that," she said. "What happened?"

"He fell off a unicycle." Bev had hoped never to have to say that to anybody.

Shirley started to laugh. "What does he do, work for the circus?"

"He fixes bicycles and things. You know, for Sears and Woolworth's, places like that."

"Bicycles, huh? Well, well." The smirk on Shirley's face seemed automatic, as if she'd been rehearsing it for years.

"So I do have to go," Bev said again, though what she really wanted was to slap this woman senseless.

"Then go," Shirley told her, flicking water into the air in a gesture of dismissal. "But I'm not leaving yet."

"Why not?"

Shirley rubbed the water droplets from her goggles and straightened her swimsuit straps. "I've got to find my wedding ring," she said. "It's in the pool somewhere."

Bev instinctively scanned the water for any faint, metallic flash, but the day was too dark for that. The pool seemed bottomless, like a fallen window of clear blue sky. When she looked at Shirley again, she wasn't sure what to think. The woman was annoying, but in spite of that Bev felt a kind of sympathy, a distant kinship that she couldn't quite name. "Are you sure it's in there?"

"Absolutely. I threw it in myself."

Bev crouched carefully by the side of the pool and pulled her wet hair back from her face. "Well, I wouldn't worry too much. It'll catch in the drain filter. You won't lose it."

"I've never had it off before. I guess that sounds pretty stupid to someone like you."

Bev had a vague sense that she was being insulted, but she didn't care. She laced her fingers together and continued to squat passively by the water. A distant roll of thunder drew her attention to the west, and as she looked out past the tennis courts toward the ninth fairway, it crossed her mind how strangely artificial the landscape was. A golf course was an unnatural thing, with its hills and rocks and trees in such manicured arrangements. Even the grass looked fake. There was something slightly depressing about it all. The land seemed flawless, but defeated—like a body laid out in a funeral home.

Shirley spotted a beetle floating by her arm and thumped it toward the deep end. "You know," she said, "I hated you in high school."

"We didn't know each other in high school."

Shirley rolled from the rope and sidestroked back to the ladder. "Didn't matter," she said quietly. "I'd look at someone like you having such a good time, dating any boy you wanted, and I felt like I was getting cheated."

"It wasn't like that," Bev said.

Shirley shrugged. "It was like that for me. I never even got asked out until the senior prom. By then I figured I was about out of chances—so I fell like a redwood for the first guy who tried to feel me up. That was Lyle, my husband. We've been together since Doomsday."

"What's wrong with that?" Bev asked. "I wish I could've found somebody when I was that young. It took me twenty years to get married."

"And still not settled down, from what I hear." Shirley pushed away from the ladder and let herself glide backward through the choppy water.

Bev's ears began to burn. "I've settled down fine," she said, though she wondered if it were true. She'd been reckless with Ed, she knew that; it didn't surprise her that people around the Club might know. The two of them had sneaked up to the stockroom a dozen times in the middle of the day when anybody might have seen them. Or maybe Ed had been shooting off his mouth—she'd known all along he was the type.

She'd been reckless with Stan, too. Right out of the blue, just sitting together on the couch one night eating popcorn, she'd told him about Ed. That much she felt good about. But she hadn't told him the affair was over, so for all Stan knew, she was still sneaking off to the stockroom every day. Why was she keeping him in the dark like that?

Shirley reached up to reset the cinch on her goggles, but she wasn't a strong enough swimmer to tread water with just one hand and had to leave the strap half fastened. Bev could see she was tiring fast—her legs moved jerkily and her breathing came shallow and quick. She seemed barely able to keep herself afloat. "You know how to tell when you're settled down?" she huffed. "It's when you feel like that's all you've ever been, like there's nothing else you could ever possibly do with your life. And that," she said, smacking her palm against the water, "is why I'm out here looking for my goddamn ring."

"So maybe you're lucky," Bev told her. "At least you've never had to be alone."

Shirley tilted her head back in the water and laughed. It was an ill-timed move for such a heavy woman. The laughter siphoned off her air, leaving her less buoyant than she realized. It didn't matter at first—the awkward flutter of her legs still held her up. But when she paused to take a breath her weight betrayed her, and before she understood what was happening her face dipped just below the waterline. She thrashed back to the surface right away, but it was too late—she came up choking, unable to take in any air. After a few frantic slaps at the water around her, she sank again.

Bev watched calmly from the side of the pool. She hated intermediate swimmers. They knew how to move themselves around in the water, but not how to stay out of trouble. They were the ones who made a lifeguard's work so tough.

In a minute she might have to do something—though not right away. Shirley was only a few yards from the ladder and still might make it back on her own. Besides, Bev's leg still ached, and her own lungs weren't altogether clear. Better to wait until things had calmed down a bit.

She tried to get a look at Shirley's face, but the rain picked up again, blurring the surface. She wondered how it felt to lose so much control—to be caught breathless underwater, swallowed in that bright silence, knowing it was up to someone else to pull you out.

Maybe Stan was feeling that right now, in surgery. Under the knife, they called it. Under the anesthetic. Maybe she would find out from him what it was like.

She sat back on the cement and fingered the wet laces of her shoes. One of them untied easily. The other had a knot, and would take a little time.

‹ ‹ ‹

Design Flaws

When the burning sensation started up again, Stan propped himself against the headboard and gingerly tugged his pajama leg up over his knee. It didn't look good.

"Hey, Bev," he called. "I think I need a hand here." He heard the oven door bang shut, but he couldn't tell if she'd slammed it or if the spring mechanism was just acting on its own. That was one of the problems with mobile homes—all the noises seemed bigger than they needed to be. Even the rain, now in its second full day, had begun to annoy him with its constant drumming on the roof and walls. Bev appeared in the doorway and leaned against the narrow frame. Her face was flushed and glistening with sweat. She carefully peeled off one of her yellow rubber gloves and ran her fin-

gers back through her hair. She looked haggard, as she often did when she was tired, but there was still something about even her tiredness that struck Stan as beautiful. He knew better than to mention it, though. She'd think he was calling her domestic and would likely slit his throat.

"What is it now?" she asked, but before he could answer she saw the problem for herself. "Christ, Stan, what did you do to it?" She pulled off her other glove and moved around the side of the bed to get a closer look.

"I think you'd better get some paper towels or something," he said. The blood had now soaked completely through the bandaging and a pair of thin red trails snaked back along his broad thigh.

"Try not to let it drip on the sheets," she said. "I'll see what I can find." She disappeared around the corner into the bathroom, and a moment later the toilet seat slammed shut. Again, Stan couldn't be sure it meant anything. Bev was a hard one to read even when he had her face to face. From the distance of another room, she was a total mystery.

"Sorry about this," he said as she emerged with a wad of toilet paper and a fresh roll of gauze. She blotted away the excess blood, then unclipped the fasteners from the elastic bandage and unwrapped the knee. She dabbed at the blood again and lifted the dressing she'd bound in place only an hour before. Stan leaned forward to help her examine the damage.

"Looks like the stitches are okay," she said, straightening

up and dropping the old gauze into the trash can by the bed. It bothered Stan that she would leave the used bandage there instead of flushing it away, but he didn't say anything. She folded her arms beneath her breasts and sighed. "You got out of bed again, didn't you?"

Stan frowned an apology. "I had to turn off the TV," he said, and nodded toward the small television perched on their dresser. "I thought if I was careful it would be okay."

Bev unrolled a strip of gauze and began to wrap his knee again. "Well, next time just leave the damned thing on."

Next time he probably would, but this time had been different. "The storm's got everything blocked out," he lied. "There was nothing but static. I couldn't listen to it anymore." He was too embarrassed to tell her he'd been frightened by a television show, a nature program on the PBS station.

"You've got to stay off this leg," she told him, tucking the end of the gauze inside the wrappings along his shin. "Every time you put weight on it, it pulls the gaps open between the stitches."

She sounded just like a nurse, Stan thought, and he wondered if that was anything she'd ever wanted to be. Probably not, since she'd never seemed to like sick people very much. Last year she'd even made him turn off the Jerry Lewis telethon because she didn't want to have to think about what it was for. At the time he'd considered that a mark against her, but now he wasn't so sure. Maybe those were the people who made the best nurses after all—the ones who wanted to get you up and out of their care as soon as possible, the ones who couldn't stand looking at the sick. Maybe Bev had missed her calling. In any case, he doubted she was happy running the snack bar at the Country Club.

"Maybe the stitches are too far apart," he offered. Doctors were just like everybody else, he figured—if they saw a shortcut, they'd probably take it.

"Maybe your brain cells are too far apart," she said. Stan didn't argue; as near as he could tell, nothing in the world was safe from a malfunction. He now knew, for example, that when baby eagles hatched, the first one to make it out of the egg tried to kill off the others by stealing their food and even shoving them out of the nest. The whole species was on the brink of extinction, and here it turned out that the biggest killer of baby eagles was other baby eagles. Where was the sense in that?

Bev bit her lip and brushed a damp strand of hair from her forehead. "I guess I'll try to rinse this out," she said, picking up the soggy elastic bandage from the bedside table. "But we'll have to let it dry before we can use it again, so don't you move a muscle. If you want something done, call me."

"I don't like to be a bother."

She held the purplish wad of elastic between her fingertips and dangled it before his face. "I'd rather change a hundred TV channels than one more of these," she said. "And we sure as hell can't afford any complications." With her free hand she drew a business envelope from her back pocket and dropped it in his lap. "If you pop a stitch," she said, "I swear to God I'll close it with a staple gun."

Stan looked down at the envelope, which had already been opened. He turned it over in his hands and saw the hospital's return address in the upper left corner. "They sure didn't waste much time," he said, but Bev was already halfway down the hall. He took out the bill and scanned the itemized list, trying in vain to decipher the column of mysterious charges. It didn't seem possible that a three-hour visit to the hospital could cost four thousand dollars. But at least now he had a fix on Bev's attitude: she was pissed.

How many bicycles would he have to assemble to pay for this? Probably about two hundred—more than three months' work. And for what? A thousand dollars for the use of the operating room—not for any supplies or equipment, which was itemized further down the list, but simply for an hour's use of the space. Two hundred more for the bed they parked him in for the hour afterward. Four hundred for drugs, antiseptics, and bottled solutions. Six hundred for surgical supplies, which as far as he could tell included only the stitching thread, some cotton balls, and his Ace bandage. They even charged him seventy bucks for physical therapy, when all they'd done was hand him a pair of crutches and tell him not to carry his weight by his armpits. The crutches themselves cost extra.

And what choice did he have—what choice did anybody

have? At least when he took his car in for repairs or had somebody over to fix his plumbing he could get an estimate first, and maybe figure how to cut a few corners. Or if he needed a pair of pants or a new toaster he could shop around for the best deal. But hospitals didn't give estimates, and they sure as hell never had a sale. He considered asking Bev to help him to the phone so he could tell them once and for all that he wasn't the king of goddamned Egypt. But Bev would think he was just being silly.

He didn't blame the hospital staff—most of them were probably no better off than he was. But he knew that somewhere behind it all, somewhere at the very back of the system in some oak-paneled office with statues in the corners, some greedy, no-good son of a bitch was calling all the shots. Whoever that guy was, he was an even bigger criminal than Stan.

Not that Stan thought of himself as a criminal, exactly. Stealing was just a sideline he'd fallen into. It wasn't as if that was all he did for a living—though the extra income would certainly take the sting out of this hospital bill. He hadn't been at it for very long—just a couple of months—and so far he'd limited all his break-ins to the Country Club, though he wasn't sure why. Maybe it was because he figured they could afford the loss. Sometimes he wished he could tell Bev about it, but he was afraid he couldn't make her understand. He didn't quite understand it himself.

Stan set the hospital bill aside and sank back into his pillow. He'd have to be careful about paying off the medical expenses. If he shelled out the whole amount all at once Bev would want to know where he got the money. He already felt himself on thin ice having to lie to her about how he'd smashed his knee in the first place. A unicycle, he told her: he was trying to test a unicycle in the product-assembly room at Sears and the thing went out from under him. "What the hell business did you have trying to ride a unicycle?" she demanded. But she never pressed him for more details. That was one handle he did have on Bev—no matter how outrageous the story, if it ended up painting him as a moron, she always believed it.

The truth was he'd been caught stealing a golf cart by some lunatic golfer who smashed his knee with a seven iron. He supposed there was a certain justice in that. In his dozen burglaries of the clubhouse and the machine shed, he'd made off with enough golf and maintenance equipment to pay for two or three knee operations. Of course, he'd also lost the dog, which he'd foolishly taken along for company one night; but on the whole he was still pretty far ahead.

Looking back at it now, he could hardly believe how much he'd managed to haul away. In the beginning, he hadn't set out to steal anything at all. On the first break-in, he'd only come away with a few golf balls and a couple of those shirts with the alligators on them—all of which he'd grabbed as an afterthought on his way out the door.

That whole night had been screwy. He remembered sitting with Bev on their couch in the living room sharing a bag of microwave popcorn. She'd seemed a little tense and sat perched on the edge of the cushion, leaning forward as if she were about to get up and leave. "Let's have a real conversation tonight," she had said. "Great," he'd answered, glad for the chance to get to know her better. They'd been married for only six months at the time, and had known each other less than a year before that, so there was still plenty of unexplored ground left between them. "You go first," she'd offered. He'd handed her the popcorn bag and laced his fingers over his chest. "I'll tell you something that bothers me," he said. "I had this dream last night, and then when I tried to remember it this morning it all just fell apart in my head. I mean, one second I knew what it was all about, and then the whole thing just evaporated. No matter how hard I concentrated, I couldn't bring any of it back. Doesn't that seem wrong to you? I mean, what's the point in having dreams if we can't remember what they are?" Stan had thought this would open up a nice conversation, but Bev had sat so still he couldn't even tell if she was breathing. "Your turn," he had said after a while. She had leaned back then to make herself look comfortable. "I'm having an affair with Ed Betzger," she had told him. "He comes to see me at work and we sneak upstairs where they keep the inventory."

Stan couldn't remember exactly what they'd said to each other after that, but he knew that somewhere along the line Bev had raised the possibility of leaving him. He remembered crumpling the empty popcorn bag and throwing it into a corner, then going out to his truck and driving away. He hadn't really been thinking about the Country Club at all, but somehow he wound up there, idling in the parking lot and staring at the darkened pro shop windows. He had tried to imagine Bev at the snack counter serving up milk shakes and candy bars to sweaty golfers and tennis players and little kids in bathing suits. But he hadn't been able to picture it, not really, because he'd never even been inside the building. He had known the snack bar was somewhere on the main floor behind the pro shop, but what did it look like, exactly? Were there tables and chairs, like a little restaurant, or just barstools lined up along the counter? Was there a rug on the floor? Were there pictures of famous golfers on the walls? Did the soft-drink fountain have Coke or Pepsi? If he couldn't answer simple questions like these, what chance did he have with the tougher ones? What chance did he have of figuring out why she set the alarm clock every night, even though they both knew the buzzer hadn't worked since their honeymoon? And why was she afraid to wear shoes with laces? And why had she been slowly filling their closets with tiny wicker baskets? How could he ever understand Ed Betzger's place in the picture when so much of the picture was still blurry? Then suddenly he had found himself knocking out a glass pane with a bicycle wrench and unbolting the lock on the pro shop door.

Maybe he could tell Bev that Sears was picking up the tab

for the surgery as some kind of part-time employee benefit program. He'd tell her he'd never read his contract too closely and hadn't realized until now that he was covered. She was bound to go for it.

He heard Bev coming down the hallway and braced himself, ready to face her with the hospital benefits story, but she stopped by the back door and swung it open into the rain. "Festus!" she called. "Here, girl!" She stood there for a long moment, long enough for Stan to consider telling her Festus was a goner; that she'd been hit by a car on the highway beside the Country Club and was now buried in a sand trap. But then he realized that the more he told her about how Festus had wound up, the more likely he was to get the blame. "I'm gonna leave this door open a while," Bev said, stepping away from the opening and turning to face him.

"Fine. It'll let a little air in here. This heat's making things pretty thick."

Bev gazed absently at him, as if he were a magazine she wasn't quite interested in finishing. He'd seen that look a lot lately. Still, maybe it wasn't a bad sign. Maybe that was the look she got when she thought about Ed Betzger. Maybe Ed's days were numbered.

What could she possibly see in that guy? He was a potbellied shrimp. Stan had seen him around town, off and on, for years, always wearing dirty white overalls and smoking a big cigar. Bev hated cigars.

What was it that made things suddenly change? When

Stan was in high school, he'd been pretty popular with certain girls because he was a big, strong guy who played football. He never had to worry about competition from little guys like Ed Betzger. But now his muscles were running to fat, and he began to realize that sheer bulk might not have the advantage in the long run. Maybe Stan was in the same boat with dinosaurs and Studebakers, and Ed Betzger was the smarter breed, the one with more of a future. After all, Betzger did have his own business. Maybe Bev thought a guy who installed cooling systems and furnaces was a better catch than a guy who assembled bicycles for department stores.

If that was the case, he could hardly blame her. When he'd first started out in bicycle repair, he'd loved his work—he didn't know of anything more graceful and sturdy than a well-built bike. But lately he'd begun to have his doubts. Something had gone haywire in the whole bicycle industry, and he wasn't sure he wanted to be a part of it anymore. He no longer trusted the basic design.

Why was it that men's bikes still had steel crotch bars between the seat and the front wheel column? Didn't anybody see how dangerous that could be? Fifty years ago it might have made sense to reinforce the frame like that, but today's bikes were more stable, the alloys were stronger. So why weren't all bicycles built like women's bicycles, with the crotch bar angled lower on the frame?

And what about the gear systems? When he'd started out assembling floor models at the Montgomery Ward store twenty years ago, the most extravagant bike they carried was a three-speed. That made perfect sense: all roads were either uphill, downhill, or flat. But then came the five-speeds, then ten, twelve, and fifteen. Now there were bicycles with more than twenty speeds. What was wrong with people that they couldn't see how silly it was to put twenty speeds on a bicycle? Didn't they know that the more complicated you made something, the more likely it was to break down? His own first bike, a bulky single-speed, had been almost indestructible. His father had even parked their old Ford pickup on it in the front yard one night. The next day, Stan had simply twisted the fenders back in place, straightened a few spokes, and ridden away like nothing had happened. These days if you just let one of the damn things tip over, it was liable to wind up in the shop for two weeks.

And why the hell had they started building handlebars upside down so you had to lean forward all the time? Whose bright idea was that? Oh, sure, maybe the aerodynamics were better—but what good was that if the ride always gave him a backache?

Bev reached out through the open door and let the rain collect in her palm, then brought her wet hand to her forehead and ran her fingers back through her hair. "It's time for your pain pill," she said. Then she shut the door and walked back toward the kitchen.

Stan shook out a couple of codeine pills from the bottle on the bedside table and washed them down with the last few swallows from his water glass. His knee didn't feel too bad right now, but he didn't want to argue with Bev about his medicine. Things were touchy enough between them already. Any wrong word might set off a fight, and he was determined not to let that happen. He didn't want to end up alone in his life, a seedy old drunkard wandering through his trailer late at night, holding up his pants. This knee problem had given him a glimpse of what lay further down the road —the pain, the stiffness, the sense that his body was trying to die away beneath him, that his life could break apart as easily as a dream. He was only thirty-nine, but already age was making him keep to the sidewalks. He ached more in the mornings than he used to, and fell more heavily into bed at night. He slumped forward when he walked, like an old man going to the library.

They'd had good times together, after all. He remembered when they'd gone out to a Chinese restaurant earlier that summer. They'd had enough to drink so that when they broke open the cookies for their fortunes, they'd laughed like maniacs at the cornball messages inside. He couldn't remember what Bev's fortune had been, but his own had stuck with him: *Persistence is not to bang ceaselessly on a closed door, but to seek out quietly the open one.* That had sounded pretty lame to him at the time; now he realized it was a fairly good description of second-degree burglary.

A sudden quiet now rose up around him: the *thunk* of the rain against the trailer had broken off. He listened hard into the stillness, waiting for the wind to whip any final shivers of rain across the roof. But the wind had died, and the only sound left was the low roll of thunder that seemed to be moving in from the south. He couldn't tell whether the storm was finally passing away or if it was just taking a breath before hitting them with whatever force it had left. As a boy, he'd loved these lulls, and used to go out into the gap between the house and the barn and wait for the wind to come shrieking back. Sometimes it was strong enough to lean into, as if it were something solid, and it tore across his body and around his ears like a swarm of ghosts.

But right now he was an almost-forty-year-old cripple in an almost-twenty-year-old mobile home, and the wind wasn't as much fun as it used to be.

"Bev," he called. "Could you come here a minute?"

She appeared in the doorway wiping her red hands on a dish towel. "I've got to be at the Club by noon," she said, "so whatever you need, ask for it now."

It hadn't occurred to him that Bev would be going to work today. "I thought you'd be staying home," he said. "The weather and all," he added.

"People still eat when it rains," she told him, slapping the dish towel over her shoulder. "Besides, they haven't given up yet on that golf tournament tomorrow. I've got to get the snack bar ready. Rod says it'll be one of our biggest weekends if the weather clears." There seemed to be a touch of enthusiasm in her voice, which made him think at once she wasn't going to the Country Club at all, but somewhere to meet Ed Betzger. He was certain they'd begun to sneak away together, though Bev hadn't said another word about Ed since she'd first broken the news. But since that night he'd begun to notice that she'd sometimes come home wrapped in odd smells. One night she reeked of motor oil, though there weren't any stains on her clothes; one night it had been something sickly sweet, like the incense they burned at the record store in town; last night she'd come in smelling like dead fish. And always there seemed to be the faint odor of cigar smoke in her hair.

But maybe he was wrong. Maybe those were the everyday smells of the snack bar. In fact, he had once tried to find out —that was his main reason for the second break-in. But he couldn't tell much—all the odors were blotted out by the pine cleaner Bev used to disinfect the countertop. It hadn't been a wasted trip, though: he'd been able to vandalize some of Ed Betzger's plumbing work in the men's locker room; and when he left, he took along a tractor mower someone had left parked beside the putting green.

Stan shifted carefully on the bed and nodded toward the high window just inside the doorway. "I was wondering what it looked like out there," he said.

Bev pulled the curtain aside and peered out through the streaked glass. "Like a trailer park," she said.

Stan knew not to rise to this particular bait. Bev hated living in a mobile home, hated being crowded in along a row of narrow tin boxes, hated the way the wind howled through the riveted seams, hated the smothering heat that pressed down from the ceiling in summer and the freeze that iced the floor in winter, hated the tiny lots strung with clothes-lines and littered with beer cans and broken toys. She hated the sounds of televisions and fights and cheap radios and squalling brats that flowed in through every window half the year. Storms were the only break from it all: then people stayed indoors with their windows closed, and the usual torrent of noises became lost in the downpour.

"It's still pretty gray," she said at last. Another low rumble began to build in the distance, and as Stan counted out the seconds to see how far away they were from the heart of the lightning, the siren in town began its long, pulsating wail. At eight seconds the remnants of the thunderclap rolled across them, sending small shivers through the walls.

"Must be a fire," he said, though he didn't believe it. A tornado warning was more likely, especially with this still-ness that had fallen over them. He wondered why nobody had thought to set up the siren so it could give different signals for different emergencies. He was sure they did it that way in other towns. Why did he always end up in the places where things were done all wrong?

The wind was rising now, whistling softly through the closed bedroom window. "I'll get the radio," Bev said, and turned back toward the kitchen as a new bank of wind broke against the front end of the trailer and echoed along the hallway. Bev clutched at the doorframe as if she expected the floor to roll out from under her. "Dammit," she said as the next sharp gust rattled the louvered kitchen windows, "I hate living in this thing."

"Relax," he told her. "The wind can't hurt us." He felt reasonably sure of that. When he'd first set the trailer on the lot, he'd anchored it with two full sets of moorings to give it more stability. Since then, trailers had been moved in on either side of them, creating windbreaks. Nothing short of an actual tornado could give them any trouble.

"I want a house," she said, and stalked off down the corridor.

"Houses shake in the wind, too, you know," he called after her. A moment later he heard the crackle of the radio and a deejay's calm voice pushing through the static. He couldn't make out much of what the man was saying, so he simply lay back to wait for Bev to bring him the news. He didn't dare try to join her in the kitchen—his knee was throbbing again in spite of the pain pills, and he knew if he tried to move there'd be more bleeding. The wind continued to butt the trailer head-on, and soon sheets of rain thrummed unevenly along the roof. Stan caught a glimpse of lightning through the thin curtains, and counted only a single second before the thunderclap hit. The deep rumble welled up through the floor and vibrated for a long moment against the paneled walls, then sank away beneath another flash and crack. The lights Bev had left on in the bathroom and the hall blinked out, and the radio stopped talking from the kitchen.

"Were we hit?" Bev asked, reappearing in the doorway. Her voice was calm, but she was rubbing her knuckles in her palm the way she did when she was nervous.

Stan smiled. "We're fine," he told her. "There's probably a line down somewhere."

Bev looked again out the bedroom window and frowned. "I don't see any lights next door."

"You wouldn't anyway, this time of day." Stan gently lifted his leg a few inches to the left and felt the pressure in his knee ease slightly. "What did the radio say?"

"There's a tornado warning until five o'clock."

Another flash of lightning filled the room, but now the thunder lagged behind, rolling in more smoothly, like a slow-moving train. "You're sure it was a warning, and not just a watch?"

"Yeah. Somebody saw one out the Fairfield Road." Bev eased herself down onto the edge of the bed and sat with her back to him. The shift of the mattress put a strain on his knee and he moved his leg slightly away from her. She turned and stared at him. "Do you want me to stay?" she asked.

Stan wasn't sure how big that question was, but he knew enough to give his biggest answer. "I'd appreciate it," he said.

Bev pursed her lips and looked down at his knee, but didn't say anything. The thunder continued to slide away toward the north, while the siren in town kept up its long, uneven whine. Finally she raised her eyes and smiled. "Can I have one of your pain pills?"

"Sure, I guess so."

She took the bottle from the bedside table, took out one of the oblong capsules, and swallowed it without water. "I'll open all the windows," she said, "so we don't get crushed like an eggshell." She brushed her fingertips along his shin and rose from the bed.

"Let's get us a place with a basement," he said. "How would that be?"

Bev moved the curtains aside and tugged at the small Plexiglas square. It moved by fits to the left until the curtain at the opened end began to snap in the breeze. "We'll probably take on some water this way," she said, and moved down the hall to the next window.

Stan didn't mind letting in the weather. The pills had begun to soften the edges of the room, and now with the wind sweeping across him and the occasional flecks of rain that reached him on the bed, he felt like he and Bev were a couple of teenagers barreling down the highway in somebody's father's car, a pair of wild kids racing through the storm.

But they weren't kids anymore, he knew that. She was a

thin, tired waitress, and he was the guy she'd settled for after twenty years of wrong numbers. Not the best framework for a marriage, maybe, but enough to work with.

Stan leaned back into his pillow and closed his eyes. Everything would be all right now. Bit by bit, they were finding where the stepstones were. She thought he was joking about getting her a house, but as soon as his leg was better, he'd go see that real estate agent who had the billboard out on Route 30. There would be enough left over from the Country Club break-ins to manage a down payment on something, he felt sure: nothing extravagant, just some nice, watertight bungalow somewhere in the country, someplace with a rec room on the lower level. Maybe he'd even get her another dog. In any case, he wouldn't let money be a problem. If Bev saw something she really liked, he'd get it for her even if it wasn't in their price range. If he couldn't handle it on the income from his bicycle contracts, he could always try a few more burglaries. Of course, the Country Club was out of bounds now. The guy who'd caught him with the golf cart must have been Bev's boss, the golf pro. Rod. Stan still wasn't too clear on why Rod hadn't called the police. Maybe he'd felt too guilty after smashing Stan's knee. Maybe he'd been worried about a lawsuit. Or maybe the guy was just an all-around screwup—that was always a possibility. But whatever the reason, Stan knew he'd just be pushing his luck if he ever showed his face around there again. He'd have to find some other place to pick on.

The hospital, for example. He'd seen all kinds of expensive gizmos there—things he didn't even have names for—and the doors stayed open twenty-four hours a day. He'd have to be careful not to steal anything dangerous—no X-ray machines or anything like that—but he was sure he could lay his hands on something, and Ric, over at Chambersburg, had promised to buy anything Stan brought in, as long as it had market value. Hell, even cotton balls and tongue depressors could earn him a few bucks at least.

Maybe wheelchairs would be the best idea. He'd never paid much attention to them before—even when the orderlies had wheeled him around after his surgery—but now he was curious about their design. Did they have gears, like bicycles? They ought to. Maybe he could think up some improvements in wheelchair mechanics and sell his ideas to one of the companies. Sure, why not? Anything was possible.

The siren seemed to rise and fall in time with the distant throbbing in his knee, and as Bev cranked open the windows at the front of the kitchen, a cool, wet wind swept through the length of the trailer. In a few minutes, he felt her crawl onto the bed beside him. She didn't say anything, but it was good to have her there, no matter what her secrets were. He wanted to touch her, to rest his hand lightly on her arm, but he was groggy now, and the codeine was dragging him away. That was all right, though. They'd have plenty of time to talk later on. Years, maybe. In the meantime, a nap would be the best thing for them both. It was the simplest way of waiting out the storm.

‹ ‹ ‹
Surface Tension

Lyle stood under the eaves of his garage and stared glumly up at the rain cascading from the roof of his house. The water twined together for the full two-story drop and smacked hard onto the edge of the crumbling driveway. Lyle wondered how the water held together like that, well defined and tangible as rope. It probably had something to do with surface tension. He remembered his high school chemistry teacher floating a needle in a glass of water and saying surface tension was what made it possible. But he never really knew what that meant. Scientific demonstrations usually impressed Lyle more as magic tricks than as examples of natural law.

Part of the overflow problem was in the sagging roofline, which dipped considerably between the end peaks of the

house and curved the guttering into what now appeared to be a thin, drooling smile. There was nothing much he could do about it. Jacking the mid-beams up would be expensive and in the short run wouldn't be worth it. He knew he could find a buyer for the place as is. The shingles still had ten years left in them, which meant he could say they had at least fifteen; and once the pigeon droppings were hosed off, the aluminum siding could almost pass for new.

The pigeons themselves, of course, would have to go. In just three weeks of roosting they'd all but ruined the carpeting on the back patio, and Lyle was sure their feathers and droppings were starting to clog the downspouts, which made the drainage problem even worse. Shirley wanted him to leave them alone—she liked hearing them coo outside the bedroom window every dawn. They were a gentle kind of alarm clock, she said. Lyle might have agreed if they'd been talking about just one or two birds. But yesterday he'd counted more than two dozen sunning themselves above the back porch. They were taking the place over. This morning at breakfast he'd tried again to get Shirley to understand the financial realities involved, but she wouldn't listen. She said that killing the birds wouldn't solve any problems. The woman simply had no head for business.

"Pigeons aren't birds," he finally told her. "They're vermin—rats with wings. They drive the property values down. If you want to live in a goddamn wildlife sanctuary, move the hell to Wyoming."

Shirley glared at him for a while, then got up from the table and put her plate in the sink. "Fine," she said, and walked out of the room.

It was settled then: the pigeons were to be disposed of. The only question was how to go about it.

A break in the downpour came just as Betzger's heating-and-plumbing van swung into the driveway. Betzger was a buzzy little cigar chewer who'd barely made it past ninth grade, and Lyle hated to be around him. He hated that Betzger always smelled of stale sweat and the undersides of toilets. He hated that whenever they talked Betzger seemed vaguely disinterested, as if he were about to say, "So what?" He even hated that such an ill-bred gnome could run his own company, drive around town in a hand-waxed van with his name stenciled neatly on the side. But business was business, and right now Betzger was one of the people Lyle had to deal with.

"What's the word, Ed?" he asked, stepping out into the drizzle as Betzger climbed down from the cab. It wasn't a casual question. He'd been on the edge of panic ever since the storm front had moved in late Tuesday night, flash-flooding his end of the neighborhood and washing out his garden. He was sorry to lose the garden because it might have been a good selling point, but what bothered him more was the rain itself. If it kept up much longer, the Member-Guest tournament might be canceled. He'd called the Country Club Thursday for some kind of status report, but none of the kids working in the pro shop seemed to know anything one way or the other. He suspected they might be lying to him, because he thought he could hear snickering in the background. Finally, though, Rod, the Club's golf pro, got on the line and told him the course was holding up pretty well. One of the practice bunkers had washed out—which Rod seemed to find particularly funny—but nothing much else seemed to be wrong. A couple of fairways were under water, which meant the gas carts would have to keep to the rough, but that wouldn't matter as far as the tournament was concerned. The rest of the course was draining well, so even if the rain held on until the weekend, everything could still come off as planned. Unless there was lightning.

"So you think I should go ahead with the clams?" he had asked.

"I can't give you any guarantees," Rod told him. "Weather is always a question mark."

"The thing is," said Lyle, trying to sound matter-of-fact, "after today it'll be too late to cancel the order."

"Yeah, well, that's a problem," said Rod. Lyle heard him bite into something, an apple maybe, or a piece of celery—something with the crunch of good nutrition. Lyle wished him dead.

After hanging up on Rod, he'd spent the rest of Thursday morning checking with the local radio stations to find out the chance of thunderstorms for the weekend. They all said the same thing: according to the wire service, the severe weather would be gone by Friday morning. The weekend would be sunny and mild.

But now it was Friday, the sky had been rumbling and cracking all day, and Lyle was stuck with a deal to take delivery on nine hundred dollars' worth of discount clams.

"Got 'em all right here," said Betzger, smiling and patting the side of his van. "Where you want 'em?"

"I hope you're not serious," said Lyle, forcing a deadpan calm into his voice.

"Just poke your head in the back and take a whiff if you don't believe me."

"But you're a day early." Lyle felt the blood beat harder in his head. "The clambake's not until tomorrow."

"Yeah, I know. The storm's played hell with the fishing schedules. None of the boats have gone out the last couple of days. Bobby said it was either this load or nothing."

"Then why the hell couldn't you wait until tomorrow to deliver it?"

Betzger shrugged. "They might not be so fresh by then. Bobby don't have anything to keep 'em cold."

So Shirley had been right. Pay retail, she had told him. If you've got to buy the stupid clams, at least get them from a legitimate outfit, and not from some fly-by-nighter like Betzger's brother-in-law. But Lyle had insisted. Clams are clams, he had told her. Now he couldn't even refuse the shipment, since he'd paid for it all in advance.

At least Shirley wasn't here to gloat. He supposed there was some consolation in that.

"And what am I supposed to do with them until tomorrow?" Lyle demanded.

Betzger looked at him as if the answer was obvious, which of course it was. "Well, if I were you," he said, shoving a fat cigar in his teeth, "I'd stick what I could in the refrigerator. The rest I'd pack in ice."

Yes, this was a reasonable solution, Lyle could see that. There was no real problem after all.

"I can rent you the ice chests," Betzger went on. "But you'll have to supply your own ice. I threw some in the back myself so the van wouldn't get too stunk up, but that's about gone now."

"Fine," said Lyle, smiling again. He felt good: he was coping now—the pounding in his head had nearly stopped. The sky was clearing, the tournament was underway, and the clams were at his door. Shirley would see that she'd been wrong.

It still amazed him that she'd been so angry about this whole affair. After all, she was the golfer in the family. Joining the Country Club had been her idea, and he'd gone along only because he figured their membership might be good for a few business contacts. So far that hadn't been the case. He didn't play golf, because it took up too much time and money; he didn't play tennis, because it involved running; and he didn't swim, because he knew what he looked like in bathing trunks. Consequently, the only person he'd actually met from the Club was a part-time busboy in the mixed lounge—a local high school kid who had no interest whatsoever in buying any houses. But when this Member-Guest thing came up, Lyle saw the potential right away. He could underwrite the clambake after Saturday's round—stage it right here in his own back yard, which was just ten minutes from the course—and turn it into a gold mine of public relations. Suddenly everyone would know who he was. Wealthy, tanned golfers would slap him on the back, extend invitations, offer him drinks. One of the boys: he'd be one of the boys.

Shirley couldn't see it. When he'd broached the subject, she'd stared at him like he was an imbecile.

"We haven't got money to throw away on a party," she said flatly. Then she picked up the *TV Guide* and began to thumb through the listings, as if the matter were already dismissed from her mind.

"Don't think of it like a party," he told her. "It's a business expense. The whole thing's tax-deductible."

Shirley closed the magazine and placed it carefully on the edge of the kitchen table. "That doesn't change the facts," she said, measuring her words as if she were speaking to a child. Then she slowly clasped her hands and leaned forward in her chair. "We can't afford to do this right now," she said.

Lyle hated it when she spoke so methodically. Somehow it made whatever she said seem indisputable. This time, though, he knew she was wrong.

"We can't afford not to," he said. "It's the best way in the world to generate new business."

"You don't know that," she said, the counterfeit of patience still shaping her voice. "All you're talking about is pure blind risk."

Pure blind risk. That was rich. Of course it was pure blind risk. His whole career was pure blind risk. That's what selling was. Why the hell didn't she know that by now? Still, he couldn't blame her for worrying about the money. The local market was tight right now; he hadn't sold a house in almost six months. But this clambake would change all that. It would buy him a million dollars' worth of visibility. What did Shirley think—that people picked their realtors from the yellow pages? Well, then she had a hell of a lot to learn. The names people trust are the names they've seen and heard most often. The basic groundwork was already laid. He had the billboard on Route 30 just outside of town, the regular ad in the Sunday paper, and free calendars to the church groups every Christmas. He wasn't unknown, not at all. But this clambake deal would make it all finally gel. He'd be back on his feet in no time. Then Shirley would smile and put her head on his shoulder and say he'd done the right thing after all.

No. He could never imagine her saying or doing anything

of the kind. That wasn't her style, not anymore. But other things were possible. First of all, she would probably demand that he replace her Volkswagen, which he'd sold to cover the cost of the clams and the beer. That would at least be a start —at least she'd be speaking to him again. Then there might be room to negotiate. That's all he needed. He was a businessman, after all, and marriage was a deal like any other. It was simply a matter of figuring the right trade-offs: this for that, this for that. The secret was in knowing how to give the small things up.

After he'd filled his refrigerator with clams and transferred the rest into coolers of cold water in the back yard, Lyle was feeling expansive enough to offer Betzger a beer, and the two of them sat down together on the rear bumper of the van. The sun by now had burned away the residual haze of the storm, and the damp air had grown muggy in the heat. The yard would have a full day to dry out, but Lyle doubted whether that would be enough.

Betzger took a long gulp of beer and tapped his foot in the broad puddle at their feet. "I notice you got a drainage problem here." He nodded toward the end of the drive. "You ought to have me dig a runoff line around this low side." He tipped his bottle toward the house. "Otherwise it'll start eating into your foundations."

"There's no place for it to run off to," Lyle told him. "We're the low point of this whole side of town. Everybody else's runoff collects right here."

"That so?" Betzger looked from the house to the street. He pointed to the sewer opening on the far curb. "What about tapping into the main line over there?"

Lyle took a sip of beer and shook his head. "Half the water in the front yard came out of that sewer. It backs up every time we get a hard rain."

"Well, you ought to do something about it," Betzger said, apparently disturbed by the thought that there was a drainage problem too difficult for him to solve. "Water don't just stand, you know. It seeps."

Lyle knew all about seepage. In the five years they'd lived in the house, he'd never known the basement to be fully dry. There was probably at least an inch of water on the floor right now, maybe more, though he'd made the conscious decision not to check. He didn't have much use for basements anyway.

"The back yard seems in good shape, though," said Betzger, frowning just enough to let Lyle know that what he was offering was not a compliment but a professional appraisal.

"Yeah," said Lyle. "The drainage is a little better there. The water seems to pool along the back property line, so most of the yard stays pretty firm."

"Where's everybody gonna sit?"

"I rented picnic tables. Hansen's is bringing them out tomorrow."

"Hansen's?" Betzger shook his head. "I could have got

you a better deal. Next time let me know. I handle all that kind of stuff for the Kiwanis Club, you know. Whatever you need, I can usually come up with it. You got the boiler and the steam tables already, I guess."

"Yeah."

"Chairs, paper plates, napkins, all that kind of stuff?"

"It's in the garage."

"How many kegs?"

"Six. We might not need that many, but we can take back what we don't tap."

Betzger sighed and took another swallow of beer. "Looks like you've got your bases covered."

More than anything in the world, Lyle wanted to believe that he had his bases covered. But something was wrong. Sellers were known by their products, he knew that. If his own home looked like a dump, who would trust him to tell a good house from a bad one?

The pond in the front yard was really no problem. All he had to do was draw attention to it himself, explain that it was some kind of freak accident. He could say one of the main sewer lines was closed for repairs and too much runoff had been rerouted his way. That would cover it. Instead of thinking he was a fool for buying a house with a drainage problem, they'd all sympathize with him, probably offer stories about when the same thing had happened to them. They'd all have a good laugh about it.

The sag of the roofline was imperceptible on sunny days

when there was no overflow in the guttering to make it obvious; and the flooded basement was a secret easily kept. But if his house was covered with pigeons, ceaselessly pacing the gutters, bobbing their heads and cooing in chorus, no one would believe he was a responsible homeowner. They'd think he was the kind of man who would let things slide, a man not to be trusted with real estate needs. Clearly, these pigeons could be his downfall.

"Know anything about pigeons?" he asked.

Betzger smiled. "They're all dark meat. Not as good as dove, though. Why?"

Lyle pointed to the roof. The pigeons had already emerged from the shelter of the eaves and were congregating around the TV antenna. "I've got some to get rid of," he said.

"Lay out a little poison," Betzger suggested.

"Too unpredictable," said Lyle. He knew he couldn't count on these birds eating whatever bait he might set out, at least not in time for them all to drop dead before tomorrow afternoon; and he sure as hell didn't want any stricken pigeons plummeting onto the patio in the middle of the clambake. "I need something quicker, something I can count on."

"Hell, plug 'em."

"Too noisy." Lyle certainly couldn't afford to make such a threatening spectacle of himself. A man who stands on his lawn taking shots at his house is not a man people will do business with. One of the neighbors might even call the police.

Betzger leaned back against the door of the van. "Well, when I was a kid me and my brother Lewis used to kill a lot of seagulls down at Rehoboth Beach. You know how they'll swoop down and kind of hover in the air, waiting for tourists to throw some bread or popcorn up in the air? We used to throw Alka-Seltzers. Birds can't belch like people, you know. All that fizz just makes them blow right up." He finished off his beer and set the bottle on the edge of the driveway. "I don't guess that'd work with pigeons, though. They can't hover, and they won't catch what you throw at 'em. But you might could toss a few Alka-Seltzers up there anyway, just for fun. Who knows? They might go for it."

Lyle tossed his own bottle into the grass. "And the next time it rained, I'd have foam all over the house."

"Well," said Betzger, squinting up toward the roof, "I could trap 'em easy enough, if you could give me a few weeks. Apart from that, there's not too many options. Bow and arrow, maybe."

As soon as the suggestion left Betzger's lips, Lyle knew it was the answer he'd been looking for. Two dozen fat, filthy pigeons skewered before sundown. He'd always been a good archer—or at least he'd always enjoyed target shooting in high school. He'd even bought himself a hunting bow for

Christmas a few years back, though he'd never gotten around to buying any arrows. The bow was still in the hall closet, waiting.

Lyle stood up and stretched. Bit by bit, the pieces of his life were falling into place. Betzger pulled a fresh cigar from his shirt pocket and bit off the tip.

"Guess I better get back to work," he said, pushing himself up from the bumper. "Let me know if you need anything else."

"I still need a load of ice. If you've got the time."

Betzger studied his watch for a moment and then nodded. "I guess I can handle that," he said. "Shouldn't take more than half an hour."

"Great," said Lyle. "Let's go."

"No need for you to come," said Betzger, pulling open the van door. "It's an easy job. I can do it just as quick by myself."

"I don't mind, really," Lyle told him. "I need to pick up a couple of things in town."

Betzger lit his cigar and turned toward the empty garage. "Something wrong with your car?"

Was there? Lyle tried to think. "It's gone," he said. "My wife took it." He remembered the fantail of water that sprang up from the street as Shirley accelerated out of the driveway. He'd never seen her that reckless before. She probably didn't realize how rocky the ride would be if she let the brake pads get wet. He might have to mention it when she got home.

"What about the Beetle?"

"We sold it."

Betzger looked surprised. "I wish I'd known," he said. "I'd have made you an offer on that car myself. Those old Bugs are getting to be real collector's items."

"Yeah, well, we sold it," Lyle said again.

Betzger shrugged. "Come on along, then. But I'll have to charge you mileage."

"Fair enough," said Lyle as he climbed in the passenger side. He truly didn't mind paying for the ride. After all, that was how a free-market system worked: supply and demand. Right now Betzger had a seller's market, and he was entitled to get whatever he could out of it. Besides, Lyle always preferred to pay for what he got. Favors made him feel uncomfortable; there were always hidden costs.

In a moment Betzger had them out on the bypass circling up to the north side of town. "Let's get some air in here," he said, cranking down his window. "Try to flush out some of that ocean stink." Lyle lowered his window and let the roar of the wind fill his head. This was nice. He could hardly hear himself think.

"So," Betzger called above the racket, "how long you figure before we get out of this slump?"

Lyle wondered if he'd missed part of a conversation somewhere, something about baseball teams, maybe. "What slump?" he asked.

"Houses," Betzger mouthed around his cigar. "Nobody's buying any houses."

"What do you know about it?" Lyle asked, a little defensively.

"Oh, I stay pretty much in touch with the market. When people buy a house they'll usually end up having a little plumbing done—either getting new stuff put in or just fixing up whatever the last owners didn't take care of. Same with central air systems and furnaces."

"So I take it you've had a drop in business lately," said Lyle, trying to steer the conversation away from his own difficulties.

Betzger nodded. "That's why I been hauling seafood for my brother-in-law. He pays me fifteen percent for deliveries. Not a bad deal. At least it's something to fall back on."

Lyle turned his face to the wind and watched the shoulder of the road blur past. Something to fall back on. That was a tactic for losers, for people who planned to fail. Falling back meant not moving forward, a life of nickels and dimes. He was glad he had nothing to fall back on. It left him no humiliating choices.

When they got downtown, Lyle had Betzger drop him off at Singleton's Sporting Goods and go on alone to pick up the ice.

"Fifteen minutes!" Betzger called after him, but Lyle was

already too preoccupied to answer. He pushed his way through the glass doors and stood breathing in the cool fluorescent air. He loved this. There was magic in retail merchandise, in the buying and selling of brand-name markups, in people making profits and customers feeling satisfied. The clean, oiled smell of it was all around him here, drawing him up and down the aisles, luring him from one display to the next, tempting him with scores of happy products he wanted but did not need—the gleam of new metal; the polish of leather; the gloss of plastic, vinyl, glass; nylon and rubber; iridescent colors; boxes stacked high. The whole scene shone with a money-back promise of sweaty, mindless play.

"Can I help you with something?" The salesman was a beefy, woodsy-looking fellow with lots of blond hair and an unforced smile. Lyle felt uncomfortable at once.

"I need some archery supplies," he said. "I've already got a bow." He added this so the salesman wouldn't take him for an easy mark.

"Target or game?"

Lyle looked down at his feet and thought hard. "Game," he said finally. "I need some arrows and a bowstring."

"How many strands?"

Lyle looked at him blankly.

"We've got ten-, twelve-, fourteen-, and sixteen-strand strings."

"What's the difference?"

"Well, if your bow's got less than a forty-five-pound

draw, you can get away with ten or twelve strands. A four-teen-strand string goes with a fifty-five-pound draw. More than fifty-five pounds and you'll need at least a sixteen-strand."

"I'll take the sixteen-strand," Lyle told him, though he had no idea if that was right.

"What length?"

"It stands about this high unstrung," he said, holding his hand at shoulder height.

"That doesn't really pin it down," said the salesman, his smile beginning to broaden. Lyle pictured him with a ski pole through his throat.

"Just give me the longest you've got," he said.

"That'd be sixty inches." The salesman reached into the glass case and selected a small package of thick black string. He set it on the countertop for Lyle's approval.

"Fine," he said. "And I'll need about fifty arrows."

"Aluminum, steel, fiberglass, or wood?"

"Which is best?"

"Well, the metal tends to hold a truer line, I think. Wood and fiberglass tend to warp when the weather changes."

"I'll take the steel, then."

The salesman opened a thick book and scanned a long row of figures. "Steels are twenty-five dollars a dozen. That's just the raw shafts. Fletching and nocking are extra. And the heads, of course."

"I see."

"Right now we're a little overstocked on helical fletching, so I could give you a good deal there."

"What about the points?"

"Well, frankly, if you take the helical fletching you can get away with a cheaper head. The torque of the arrow gives you maximum penetration out of a simple target point. If you go for the four-sided blade heads, the point itself will keep the arrow on true flight. So you don't really need as much rotation. But it depends on what you're going after. If it's a bear, you want as nasty a head as you can find. If it's a rabbit, you can get by with something a lot simpler, maybe even a blunt point for stunning."

"I want the big heads," Lyle told him. "The ones that look like razor blades."

"I can let you have those for two dollars apiece." He made a few notations on his receipt pad. "How about some camouflage gear?"

"No, I don't think so. I'll just use my old marine fatigues." He had no marine fatigues.

"How about cover-up and lure."

"What do you recommend?"

"Pine oil's a pretty popular cover-up. Some people use skunk oil, but I think that'll make a deer or whatever suspicious. Skunks don't spray unless there's trouble around, and animals know that. But personally I'd go with small-animal urine. It's cheap and it's natural." He took a small bottle down from a shelf behind the counter and offered it to Lyle.

"I don't want animal urine," he said. He was sure of this.

The salesman returned the urine to its place on the shelf and took down a smaller plastic squeeze bottle. "How about standard rut lure, then? If deer's what you're after. Lay a track of this stuff through the woods and bucks will follow you for days. All you've got to do is wait for them to catch up and then show them what Cupid's arrow can really do."

Lyle began to feel sick. "I'm not after deer," he said. "I just want to sell some houses."

The ride back was pleasant. Loading thirty-five bags of crushed ice into the van had apparently worn Betzger down enough to dull his interest in conversation, so Lyle had nothing to do but smile happily ahead, the sack of arrows clutched to his chest. When they pulled to a stop in the driveway, Lyle climbed down from the truck and headed immediately for the house, leaving Betzger to unload the ice by himself. Lyle didn't feel guilty: he knew Betzger would charge him plenty for the extra work, and right now time meant more to him than money. The sun was already starting its descent; in another two hours the glare would be directly in his eyes as he sighted on the birds. He could shoot only from the front yard, after all, since the weed lot bordering the back yard was the only place he could drop the arrows safely. He knew he wouldn't get every pigeon this afternoon, but at least he'd have a good head start on tomorrow.

The arrows, it turned out, were easy to assemble, and it wasn't until he'd finished the last one and set it on the pile that he realized fifty arrows was more than he needed. Any misfires could be easily retrieved and shot again. Still, this way would be more convenient, so he didn't feel bad. And luck was with him on the bowstring. He'd planned to tie knots in it to shorten it for his bow, but it turned out he'd bought the right length, after all. He bent the bow around the back of his leg like a veteran archer and looped the loose end of the string over the notches. Everything was ready. He gathered the bundle of arrows under his arm and slung the bow across his chest as he'd seen it done in the movies. Then he slipped quietly out the back door, thinking to circle around and catch his prey off guard. Betzger had emptied the ice bags into the clam coolers, he noted, and as he rounded the corner of the house he realized the van was gone. He felt oddly alone, as if he'd just been left in the wilderness on a two-week survival course. He stopped for a moment to listen: the neighborhood was quiet except for the faint whir of a distant lawn mower and the trilling coo of the pigeons.

He eased out toward the middle of his front lawn and looked up at the gallery of birds ranged along his roofline. They were all watching him. For the first time he noticed their feathers. Each bird was distinctively glossed with iridescent swirls of color—not like most birds, which seemed merely to be interchangeable versions of one another. Some of these pigeons were beautifully marked. Shirley had mentioned that once, he now recalled. She'd even given some of them names. Albert. Red. Scruffy. Slick. Marjorie. Lyle didn't want to remember which was which.

It had been a long time since he'd used a bow, and it occurred to him that he ought to aim a little high for the first few shots, just until he got his accuracy back. No sense ripping up his shingles. But beyond that single precaution, he realized he had no real strategy of attack. With geese, he knew, it was smart to shoot the birds at the end of the flying formation first so the others wouldn't panic and spread. He doubted whether the same principle applied here, but something about his sense of order told him to start from the left and work his way across, the way he would in a shooting gallery.

Lyle positioned himself so his sight line ran parallel to the slant of the roof and drew back the bow for his first shot. He held the pose for a moment, focusing on a blue-and-white bird that had paused by the chimney to watch him. He let the arrow fly and watched it soar quickly out of sight. The pigeon seemed undisturbed. Good power, Lyle told himself, not worried that the first shot had failed to come within a yard of the target. He was just finding the range, after all.

The second arrow came no closer than the first, though

this time the pigeon hopped and fluttered a bit, as if it now suspected something was up. Lyle pulled the bow back as far as he could and sent a third arrow whizzing toward the roof-line. The shot was wide to the right, but another bird blundered up over the crest at just that moment, and the arrow caught him right below the beak, completely removing his head. He flopped forward and tumbled down the incline, snagging briefly on the guttering before a final spasm propelled him over the edge and onto the boxwood in the yard below. Lyle stepped up and looked at the headless bird lying cushioned by the springy branches: it was Slick, his colors still shimmering on his back like the rings of an oil spill.

Lyle felt vaguely disturbed, as if he were a trespasser in his own front yard. The accidental nature of the kill made it all the more grotesque, and now every thought in his head seemed suddenly shameful and unnatural. He needed Shirley here, to tell him what was wrong.

The other pigeons seemed largely unconcerned. A few rose and flapped to the top of the chimney or circled away to the rear of the house, but most stayed right where they were.

Lyle eased out farther in the yard to get a better angle against the increasing glare and set another arrow to the bowstring. Again he pulled the bowstring back as far as he could, bringing the silvery blades of the head almost to his fingers. He leveled his aim on a stark white bird perched on the gutter by the downspout, a bird Shirley had not yet named. For a long moment Lyle held the pigeon in his sights, staring up the shaft to the round, plump breast. A tightness crept through his arms and across his chest, and suddenly he'd waited too long, the strain was too great, the bow began to quiver. Still, he held the arrow back, his fingers tight against the string, so tight they hurt, so tight a numbness took them over, freezing them in place, as if they weren't a part of him at all. He took a sharp breath and strained again against the bow, and now his fingers unlocked, the bowstring snapped away, and the arrow flew up hard against the house, the head slicing through the aluminum siding.

The pigeons rose with a start and swept away to the stand of trees beyond his neighbor's house, disappearing quietly into the topmost branches.

Lyle stared hard at the ruined siding, unable to believe what he'd done. But there it was, the feathered shaft protruding from his outer bedroom wall. How could he explain a thing like that? What would Shirley say?

He dropped the bow and walked to the edge of the porch where he could better gauge the damage. The arrow was in deep, and he guessed the razored head would be sticking through the plaster just above the picture Shirley had hung on that wall—the small, blurry photo of the two of them on the beach at Dauphin Island. It was the only picture they had from their honeymoon, taken by a man with a Polaroid who'd charged them two dollars. Their own camera had been lost when the sailboat Lyle had rented capsized in choppy water.

He knew she had always blamed him for that, and re-membering it now, he supposed he hadn't used his best judgment. He had wanted to impress her, but he'd never sailed before and, without realizing what he was doing, he steered the boat broadside to the wind. Lyle managed to scramble up over the side of the boat as it rolled, but Shirley had gone into the water with the mast on top of her and for a moment she was held under, caught beneath the sail. But only for a moment—Lyle pulled her out, then righted the boat and drew her back on board. "We're all right," he told her, but she was hysterical and slapped his hands away. She said he had no business taking them out where a thing like this could happen. He was surprised she could be so furious and kept silent as he maneuvered the craft toward shore, worried the whole way back that he might tip them over again. They were both relieved when the hull finally scud-ded into the soft updrift of the beach, but for a long time neither of them moved from the boat, or even spoke. "It was just an accident," he said at last. "That's no excuse," she told him. Why wasn't it? he wondered, though he felt afraid to ask.

Now she would see this arrow as one more piece of evi-dence against him. It wasn't fair. She had no right to blame him for things he'd never meant to do. But she would blame him, and now he felt more guilty than if he'd shot the house on purpose. His face felt chilled, as if he'd run too far, too fast, and turned his sweat cold. He could feel the blood beating in his head.

He had almost mustered the courage to go inside when Shirley wheeled their Plymouth through the pool of water at the foot of the driveway and pulled up in front of the garage. There was no use pretending he hadn't seen her—she'd only get suspicious—so he sat casually on the edge of the stoop and waited for her to join him.

"Hello," she said. Her face was still pretty, even without a smile.

"Hi." He liked her dress. It was blue with little flecks in it, like a robin's egg.

"I came back to get some of my things." He liked her gold earrings, too, but they made her look too formal for this time of day. Her hair—was there something different about her hair? He couldn't tell.

"Sure," he said. "Fine."

She sighed and walked past him into the house.

Lyle couldn't believe his luck. Slick was lying right there, headless, in the branches of the boxwood and she hadn't even noticed. He didn't think she had seen the bow and arrows, either. If he could just get everything out of sight, she might never know what he'd been up to. Of course, she was bound to see the arrow in the bedroom wall, but when she asked him about it, he could act surprised. "Must have been vandals," he would tell her. Kids today were just that crazy—she'd have to believe him. Sure, everything would work out fine.

He shoved the bird deep inside the bush and hurried out into the yard to gather the equipment. The sewer was a likely place, especially for the arrows; he wasn't sure whether the fiberglass bow would float or not, but figured he could stuff it far enough down the opening so that it wouldn't matter.

As he waded along the curb, feeling for the storm drain with his feet, he kept an eye on their bedroom windows. There was no sign of Shirley. He smiled. She had probably decided to start fixing dinner. In a little while she would open the door and call him inside for roast beef, carrots, and mashed potatoes. He would say something nice to her then, maybe ask about her hair. By then he would have everything back under control. She would never suspect a thing.

‹ ‹ ‹

Torch Song

Rod could tell there was going to be a fight. He was too far from the pool table to hear the particulars—especially now that the band had launched into its second set, drawing a dozen of the tavern's cheering drunks back onto the cramped dance floor—but the story seemed clear enough through body language alone. The big guy in the denim jacket was apparently hogging the table, and the thin punk slouched against the cigarette machine was giving him a hard time about it. Not a smart idea, in Rod's view. The big guy had a rough, rawboned look, like he'd just climbed out of a ditch. His fat hands were darkened with some greasy residue —engine oil, maybe—and Rod imagined him to be a biker, since the weather was otherwise too hot for the jacket. His

hair was uncombed, his face unshaven, and his clothes unwashed.

After each shot, the punk sneered and muttered some remark, sometimes stepping away from the cigarette machine to point a threatening finger in the big guy's face. He seemed oblivious to the risk he was running, to the fact that he was outweighed by maybe a hundred pounds and could be snapped like a golf tee if he forced things too far. He acted like one of those small, high-strung dogs Rod hated so much—the kind that would bark and snap at his ankles until he couldn't help but want to kick it through a wall.

At the same time, Rod felt oddly sympathetic toward the punk. At first he couldn't figure out why—the guy was clearly a jerk and in his own way every bit as unsavory as the biker. He had a liar's look, shifty-eyed and cold, and his lip curled up on one side as if he'd just tasted something bitter. His black T-shirt was too small for him, the tightness probably calculated to make the stringy muscles of his arms and torso stand out. Intricate blue-green tattoos stretched along both his pale forearms, though Rod was too far away to make out the designs. The man looked both anemic and wild, like some animal brought up from the cellar.

But there was still that something: a thing that forced Rod to stare hard until he'd figured out what his connection was with this guy. When the answer finally came to him, it was unsettling. The punk by the pool table was a loser in every visible way; he was also a dead ringer for Rod.

Not that Rod looked like a loser. He was a golf pro, after all, suntanned and robust—not some low-life tavern thug. His hair was neatly trimmed, and his clothes were casual but expensive, color-coordinated in all the right pastels. He had a certain standing in the community. No, he and this punk were like opposite sides of a coin. But they did share the coin, there was no denying that, and there was only one face between them.

The big guy was obviously smoldering, his cheeks flushing redder with each round of heckling, but he kept his eyes on the table, sinking half a dozen balls before finally scratching on a bank shot. Then the guy with Rod's face said something to his buddies hovering in the background, and they all laughed. That seemed to do it for the biker, who threw his cue to the floor and started around the table toward them. The punk stiffened to meet him, and Rod's stomach tightened with a surge of helplessness and dread that felt like tires skidding on a highway just before a crash.

But then it stopped: there was no collision. Two steps short of what could have been murder, the big guy caught himself, turning suddenly self-conscious, wary, as if he'd blundered into a spotlight before an unfamiliar crowd. He glanced surreptitiously over his shoulder—not toward Rod but toward the bar, where the burly bartender leaned forward on one elbow, watching, his right hand absently rolling the heel of an aluminum baseball bat back and forth across the counter, keeping time to the rhythms of the band.

The biker took a long breath and gazed around the room, apparently thinking things over. The punk stood frozen like a cartoon pug, chest out, jaw set, and fists clenched as if he still expected a charge, but the biker just nodded to him now and turned away. He downed the last third of his beer, set the mug carefully on the end of the bar, and strolled out the door.

The room seemed much less crowded now. The bartender put away his bat, and the punk at the pool table strutted from pocket to pocket, retrieving the balls for a fresh rack, while his friends inspected a few cue sticks for warp. The band eased into a slow, smoky number, a showcase, it seemed, for the redheaded singer in the low-cut gown, and the dancers drifted like sleepwalkers back to their cluttered tables.

Rod took a healthy gulp of his whiskey sour, hoping it might ease the knotted muscles in his neck. Maybe coming here had been a bad idea. He'd never been much of a barhopper, and in the four years he'd been the pro at the Country Club, this was the only tavern he'd ever frequented. The last time he'd been here, he'd met the woman who sang with the band—had been stung by her, in fact. Still, when Harold Hanshaw called and pressured him into getting together for a drink, no place else had come to mind.

But what the hell did Harold Hanshaw want with him anyway? He barely knew the guy. He'd seen him only four times in as many years—always at the Member-Guest golf tournament, where Harold played with his father, Glen L. Hanshaw, the Club president. Rod wasn't even sure he could recognize Harold outside the context of the pro shop. That was partly why he'd made a point of coming half an hour early, so Harold would be the one who had to pick a face from the crowd. But he also wanted a chance to get used to the place before Harold showed up—a chance to grow comfortable in the tavern atmosphere, maybe strike up a conversation with someone in the band. A golfer's habit, really—studying the course before playing the round. But it was no use; even after two whiskey sours, he still couldn't imagine what this meeting was about. And the woman across the room, caressing the microphone and crooning her throaty version of some half-familiar country song, still hadn't noticed him at all.

She didn't sound quite as heavenly or as desperate as the last time, when he'd been more drunk, but she still had that raw, doomed quality in her voice that seemed to pull her inside the music, down to a place where breath and heartbeat stopped. For Rod, each note she sang took on a melancholy shape he'd known before, echoing back across the years to someplace in the starry darkness of a single teenage night. He could have listened for hours.

A barmaid paused by his table and picked up his empty glass. "Can I get you another?" she asked. There was a hint of impatience in her voice, as if she were telling him his time was up, and Rod suddenly realized he was monopolizing three empty chairs at his table while other patrons—a wave of recent arrivals—clotted around the bar with no place to sit.

"I'm waiting for someone," he told her, but when he realized he hadn't answered her question he added, "Bring me two more whiskey sours."

She chewed the inside of her cheek. "You mean a double or two drinks?"

"Two drinks. One for my friend," he said, nodding to the empty chair across from him. He felt like an idiot. She scribbled something on her pad and moved away toward the bar.

As the singer faded into the finish of her song, she seemed to slide from country into something more like roadhouse blues, repeating some mournful but unrecognizable phrase in softer and softer tones, rounding the vowels and slurring the hard consonants, like a drunk slipping deeper into a dream. When the last note died away, an appreciative silence lingered for a moment throughout the room, then vanished with the crack of billiard balls and the voice of the man with Rod's face whooping at the good fortune of his shot. The woman glanced involuntarily toward the pool table, then bowed her head to the smattering of applause. Rod thought he saw a flash of anger in her eyes, though he might have been mistaken.

The next song was more upbeat, and since the lead guitarist and the guy on keyboards seemed to be handling the vocals, leaving the woman with little more than an occasional bar of background harmony, Rod found his attention drifting back to the pool table. It was odd to see himself playing pool like that, lighting up menthol cigarettes, popping the knuckles of his left hand, scratching his tattoos, laughing with a strange set of friends. But that's what it was like: seeing himself—though cast into a different life, as if he'd stumbled upon a fun-house mirror that somehow changed everything about him but his looks. The longer he watched, the more he felt connected—not to this punk knocking balls around a table, but to something outside himself, a world of untapped possibilities, options he'd never known he'd had. He felt blessed, like he'd hit a bad drive but a freak wind had saved it, steering the ball inexplicably across the water and onto the green.

The barmaid set the whiskey sours on the table, one in front of Rod and the other at the empty place across from him. "That'll be six-fifty," she said, pushing her voice above the music.

He handed her a ten. "Keep the change," he said, smiling, and she smiled back, a small concession. It was the opening he'd hoped for. "Listen," he said, "could you do me a favor?" He took out a pen and scribbled a note on his cocktail napkin, then folded it carefully and handed it to her. "Would you give this to the woman who sings with the band?"

She looked suspiciously at the napkin, then back at Rod, sizing up his intentions. "Brenda doesn't do requests," she said.

"No, that's not it. I might have some work for her. For the whole band."

She unfolded the napkin and read Rod's note back to him. *"Please join me. I have a proposal."* She shook her head. "Seems a little vague to me. Sounds like you might want to marry her."

"That was meant to be a private message," Rod said.

She smiled sweetly. "Well, I guess that kills my career with the Post Office." She dropped the napkin back onto the table and moved away through the crowd.

Rod didn't know whether to be angry or embarrassed. He considered following her to the bar to explain himself, but realized if he got up, he'd lose his table. Besides, even if he figured out what he wanted to say, she wasn't the woman to say it to. For weeks now the redhead with the band had haunted him. *She* was the one he had to pour himself out for.

He had no idea why. He knew it was crazy, that he was acting like those deranged fans who stalk movie stars or make regular pilgrimages to Graceland. But something about this woman seemed to promise him things. He could feel it in her songs.

Maybe the barmaid was on to something: maybe he did want to marry her. Maybe that was just the kind of shake-up he needed. Why not? Even from a distance he could see that this beautiful and possibly heartbroken woman, this Brenda, was nothing like his first wife, and that had to be a good sign. Why not just leap blindly toward a possibility for once? Why not restart his life as some kind of stranger? Not the stranger at the pool table, but someone just as alien—someone willing to risk the out of bounds for the sake of extra yardage; someone who didn't mind playing from the rough.

"Pretty crowded in here." The fat man smiled down at him expectantly.

"All right," Rod told him. "You can take one of the chairs, but I still need the table."

The man's smile drooped in confusion, and Rod immediately realized his mistake. "Sit down, I mean. Have a seat."

Harold Hanshaw eased himself into the chair across from Rod. "Is this for me?" he asked, indicating the drink.

"Yeah. They had a special on whiskey sours."

"I'll have to pass," Harold said, easing the drink aside with the back of his hand. "Doctor says I've got to lay off the alcohol for a while. He thinks I'm gonna have a stroke."

"Well, I'm not," said Rod. He picked up Harold's cocktail and poured part of it into his own half-empty glass. Why the hell would Harold ask him out for a drink if drinking was off his list?

Come to think of it, was this even Harold? All the middle-agers looked pretty much the same to him at the Club. Not that they looked alike, exactly, not the way Rod and the guy at the pool table did. But they all seemed to blur together in his mind, like cattle.

Maybe his first wife had been right. Maybe he ought to look for some other line of work, something outside of golf. He still loved the game well enough—that wasn't the problem. He just always seemed to hate the people who played it.

"I'm glad you could make it tonight," Harold said. "I was afraid you'd be too busy with the tournament."

"Friday's pretty much a free night for me," Rod said. He took a swallow of his drink and scanned the crowd. Hunters, he guessed, for the most part. A couple of fly fishermen. Maybe a few bowlers. "How'd you hit 'em today?"

"Too often," Harold said, mopping his forehead with a cocktail napkin. "I couldn't break an egg. The course is still pretty wet."

"Well, today was just the practice round. It ought to be a lot drier out there tomorrow."

Harold leaned slightly forward and folded his hands together on the tabletop like he was about to say grace. "I don't want to talk about golf," he said. "I wanted to talk to you about my father."

"He's a great guy," Rod lied. "His handicap's up this year. With a little luck, you guys could walk off with some prizes."

Harold frowned at the tabletop. "I think there's something wrong with him. He's not acting right."

Rod shrugged. "You know him better than I do."

"But you see him more often."

"I see him around the clubhouse. Maybe his golf game's a little off, but apart from that he seems pretty much the same as ever. Still more gristle than fat."

"Well, he's not the same," Harold insisted. "What about those mules? You know about that, don't you?"

Rod knew about the mules. Over the past few months Glen Hanshaw had been buying up all the derelict mules in the county. He kept them in his back yard, which bordered the golf course, and all summer long golfers had complained about the noise and the smell. Rod had never brought the matter up before the Board, though. Crazy or not, Glen still ran things at the Club and would have fired him on the spot.

"Maybe he just likes mules," Rod said. The room fell briefly quiet as the band finished another set. Rod tried to get a glimpse of Brenda through the crowd, but too many dancers had been left stalled at his end of the dance floor.

Harold tapped his index finger urgently on the table as if he were punching the buttons of a calculator. "He says things that don't make sense. He forgets who people are." He fluttered his hand strangely in the air. "Three times today he called me Benny. Benny's his *cat*, for God's sake." He shook his head. "I was thinking maybe I might have to do something. You know, for his own good."

Rod took a swallow of his whiskey sour. "I don't know,

Harold. Your dad's a pretty tough knothole. I wouldn't write him off too early."

Harold seemed to swell in his chair, ready to spill out all the arguments he'd marshaled against his father. "It's not about being tough," he said. Then he stopped, abruptly, like a dog caught chewing on the tablecloth, and stared past Rod at some dance-floor distraction. Rod turned in his seat, half expecting to find Glen Hanshaw shoving his way through the crowd, come to box poor Harold's ears for trying to stick him in a rest home. But it wasn't Glen he found standing by his chair. It was Brenda.

"I don't mean to interrupt," she said, "but Marcie says you want to see me." She looked from Harold to Rod, apparently uncertain which of them she was talking to.

"Yes," Rod said, getting to his feet. "I do." He pulled out the chair beside him. "Please, have a seat."

She eyed him closely. "She also says you're probably a jerk, and I shouldn't waste my time listening to you."

"I might want to hire your band," he said.

"Yeah, Marcie told me." She glanced toward the pool table and lowered herself stiffly onto the chair, careful not to strain against the too tight fit of her dress. "Okay," she said, "I guess I can listen."

"I'm Rod Dale," he said, offering his hand. She took it reluctantly, as if he were handing her a fish.

"Brenda Glass." Her lips puckered slightly as she scrutinized his face. "You look kinda familiar," she said.

"I've been here before. A few weeks ago. You mistook me for somebody else."

Her face opened into a smile. "Oh God, I remember. You're the guy I thought was Randy." She put her fingers to her mouth and shook her head. "You musta thought I was crazy."

"Not at all."

She dipped her head toward him and spoke in a half-whisper. "The truth is, I was pretty loopy that night." She was also pretty loopy right now: her eyes were dilated to the size of golf balls, giving them a black and vacant look. This was a woman who could crack his heart as casually as she would a walnut. But that was the point, or as near as he could fathom it. His life had gone stale as bread crusts, and she was the beautiful wrong woman, the disaster he desperately needed to slap himself awake again.

"Would you like a drink?" he asked.

The offer seemed to pain her. "I better not," she said. "I'm fine like I am."

"That's a rare state," said Harold.

"Oh, and this is Harold Hanshaw," Rod said. Harold nodded morosely and pretended to study his cocktail napkin.

She raised an eyebrow. "Hanshaw? Any kin to the Cadillac dealer?"

"Same family," Harold said. "But I can't get you a discount."

"Discount?" Her eyes flashed. "You couldn't *pay* me to

take a car off that lot. I got ripped off by you guys once before. You sold me a used Pontiac Astre. The engine block cracked about four days after I got it home."

Harold sighed. "Must've been one of the old aluminum-block models. They had all kinds of trouble with those. The Chevy Vega caught most of the flak, but the Astre was just as bad. It was the same damn car, in fact, only with a different name plate."

"Well, that's a real comfort to know," she said.

"Look, don't blame me for your car troubles. My father runs the dealership. I don't have anything to do with it."

"Harold's an accountant with the state," Rod said.

Harold looked surprised. "Who told you that?"

"Your father, I guess."

Harold rocked back in his chair and ran his palms across his bald head. "Jesus, that's exactly what I'm talking about. I quit that job fifteen years ago. I've got a product design firm now."

"What's that?" asked Brenda.

Harold seemed to turn the question over in his mind. "Well, I guess it's market research, mostly," he told her. "Cut-rate department stores hire us to design the packaging for their in-house brands. Basically, the idea is to make *their* shampoo look just like the other guys' shampoo."

"I don't see much point in that," she said.

Harold chuckled. "You would if you saw the sales figures. People tend to reach for packages they recognize. If we can make some off-brand look just like the market best-seller, people are more likely to buy it." He wiped the side of his hand across the tabletop, sweeping a trail of pretzel crumbs to the floor. "It's kinda fun, really—almost like a game. You've got to play all the angles." He looked across at Rod, and a weariness crept into his face. "Jeez," he said, "I can't believe my father still thinks I'm a goddamn accountant."

Rod leaned over and touched Brenda lightly on her bare forearm. "Harold thinks his father might be getting a little senile."

"It happens," she said.

"Exactly right," Harold agreed. "It happens. And when it does, people ought to do what they can to help."

"Sure, but it's not that simple," Rod said. "I mean, what do you want me to do? Tell some judge your dad's incompetent and ought to be locked up?"

Harold shifted sideways in his chair. "You say that like it's a bad thing. Look, I'm just worried he's gonna hurt himself, that's all. I thought maybe his friends would back me up on this."

"Harold, your father's a great guy and all, but I'm not really what you'd call one of his friends. I'm more like an employee."

Brenda frowned. "You work at the car lot?"

"I'm the golf pro out at the Country Club," he told her.

"Like there's a difference," Harold said, turning away toward the bar.

Brenda leaned close enough for Rod to smell her perfume. It was something floral and sweaty. "Is that where you want to book us?" she asked. "The Country Club?"

"Yeah. The Club has dances every month. So far it's been mostly polka bands—"

"My dad loves polka music," said Harold. "He thinks it's zippy."

"—but the younger members want something a little more contemporary. Like the stuff you do."

Brenda chewed delicately on her thumbnail. "We're not really what you'd call contemporary," she said. "Some of our country stuff is pretty recent, but most of our rock is from the sixties. And my torch songs are a lot older than that."

"That's great," said Rod. "That's perfect."

She leaned forward on her elbows, and Rod made a half-hearted effort not to stare down the top of her dress. "So what you need, basically, is something non-polka."

"Right. That's what we need. Non-polka."

An almost sleepy amusement crept into her eyes. "Yeah, I guess we could handle that."

"Since when have you got the authority to hire new bands?" asked Harold. "I thought that was something the Board had to decide."

"I'm chairman of the dance committee," he lied. "All the nominations have to come through me." He smiled at

Brenda. "And as far as I'm concerned, the nominations are closed."

Harold began to tear his napkin into thin strips. "Yeah, right. You sound just like my brother Bill. He always pretended he could do things his own way. But somewhere along the line my father always stepped in and reminded him who really called the shots."

Rod sipped at his drink. "I didn't know you had a brother," he said.

Harold paused as if to think this over. "Well, I don't anymore. People still talk about him, though. He stepped off the water tower the summer after he graduated from high school."

"Oh God, I remember that," said Brenda.

"Yeah," said Harold. "Everybody does. Except maybe my father. Pretty ironic, if you ask me." Harold plucked a piece of ice from the extra whiskey sour glass and slipped it into his mouth. "People thought it was an accident because he had a can of spray paint with him. But the can was already empty when he took it up there. I figure that was his suicide note. Bill always had an offbeat way of doing things."

"Look," said Brenda, straightening in her seat, "we'd like to play the Country Club—assuming the dates are clear and the money's okay—but maybe we shouldn't talk about it until you can give us something in writing."

"I can do that now," Rod insisted. "I've got the papers in

the car." For all he knew, he wasn't lying. His car had long been the graveyard for all his unfinished paperwork; surely he could improvise a contract from the wealth of debris in his trunk. It wouldn't take much—a stack of invoice blanks, maybe, or a fresh pad of purchase orders—anything generic enough to support some kind of agreement.

Brenda looked at her watch. "I've got to start another set in a few minutes," she said.

"I'll get the contracts right now," he said, getting up from the table. "We can get everything settled."

He pushed his way quickly through the crowd and walked out the door into the yellow glow of the parking lot. He trotted to his car and popped open the trunk. Jackpot: there were order forms everywhere. Most of them had various company logos at the top, but he knew he could work around that. He shoved his golf bag aside and rifled through the pile for a likely document.

He'd just fished out a pad of requisition blanks from the Izod sportswear company when something slammed into him from behind, pitching him forward and driving his brow into the steel edge of the trunk lid. White flashes burst across the inside of his skull, after which he felt suddenly detached, upended by a sense of separation, of two halves jarred loose from one another. His body sagged beneath him, stunned into momentary uselessness; but his mind seemed merely to stand aside and watch, like a curious bystander at an unscheduled fireworks display. His first clear thought was that he'd been hit by a car, but that guess faded as a fierce grip clamped into his shoulder and jerked him violently around. A large hairy face floated in front of him, but he couldn't quite bring it into focus. Maybe he was being mauled by a bear.

"Ric, wait a minute. That's not him." The voice came from a shadow floating a few feet behind the bear. "Look at his clothes, man. That's not him."

The bear pulled Rod up close and frowned into his face. "Son of a bitch," it said. "You're right. Looks like I really rang this guy's bell, too." The bear gave an embarrassed laugh and eased Rod back against the lip of his trunk, propping him in place like a broken doll.

"Hey, buddy," said the shadow, moving forward now and slapping him lightly on the cheek. "Hey, buddy, are you okay?"

The landscape began to reassemble itself around him. "Jesus Christ," Rod groaned, touching his hand to the lump rising on his forehead.

"Hey, I'm real sorry," the big man told him, leaning in close and curling a protective arm around Rod's shoulder. "I tripped and fell right into you. That musta really hurt."

"Forget it—no problem," he said, cupping his palm gently over the swelling. "I'm fine." He squinted up at the two men. The smaller guy, the shadow, was a stringy young greaser he'd never seen before, but the other one, Ric the Bear, was easy to recognize. He was the biker Rod had seen playing pool. "I'm fine, really," he said again. "I just need to sit here a minute."

"Sure, that's it," said Ric cheerfully. "You take it easy. Get yourself some aspirin, you'll be fine." Ric grinned at his partner, then the two of them ambled away across the dusty lot and took up posts on either side of the tavern's main exit, lounging like bored gargoyles against the dark brick wall.

Rod took a few slow breaths. His head throbbed, but at least he felt like himself again. The Izod requisition pad was still clutched in his right hand, and as he stared down at it he remembered what had brought him outside in the first place. He folded the top of the form in a sharp crease and carefully tore away the part with the company logo, then closed the trunk and steered himself shakily across the parking lot. At the tavern door both gargoyles nodded politely.

"Looks like everything's fine," Ric said.

Rod smiled weakly. "No harm, no foul, I guess." He pulled open the door and walked back inside. He'd only been gone a couple of minutes, but the ache in his head made the place seem different now. The air was too stale, the room too crowded, the laughter too loud, the floor too messy with spilled drinks and cigarette butts. His table seemed much, much further from the door.

When Rod reached his chair, Brenda and Harold were sitting in an awkward silence. One of them had finished off Harold's whiskey sour.

"What the hell happened to you?" Harold asked. "We thought you got carried off by Gypsies."

"I hit my head on the trunk lid," he said, unfolding the order blank and handing it to Brenda. "It slowed me down."

Harold shook his head. "Christ, no wonder you think my dad's normal. You both need a goddamn nanny."

"This doesn't look like any contract I've ever seen," Brenda said, studying the printed sheet. "It looks like some kind of invoice."

"That's how we set things up," Rod assured her. "We use this form whenever we need to requisition funds from the Board. Golf balls or dance bands, it all comes out of the goods and services account."

Brenda chewed her lower lip for a minute, then turned to Harold. "You probably know about these things. Is this a legit contract or not?"

Harold glanced at the form. "It'll do," he said. "As long as you've got a place for the signatures, you can write a contract on the side of a cow."

Brenda smiled. "Well, all right, then," she said, putting her hand over Rod's. "Let's talk about some dates."

"Well, don't you two look cozy."

Brenda withdrew her hand and looked up at the man now standing across the table from her. "Randy," she said. "Hi, sweetheart."

He stood glowering at Rod for a moment, then turned

his stare back to Brenda. "You're on a pretty long break," he said.

"We're having us a little business meeting," she said brightly. "Rod wants to hire the Radio Actives for some of the dances at the Country Club."

"Rod, huh?" He stepped over the back of the empty fourth chair and sat down heavily, like a teenager. But he wasn't a teenager, that was obvious. Mid-twenties, Rod guessed, though he didn't care to look too closely. "How much is he gonna pay?"

"We hadn't got that far yet. I was thinking maybe"—she glanced tentatively at Rod—"five hundred dollars?"

"Seven," said Randy. "It's seven or no deal."

"Are you the band's manager?" Rod asked.

"I'm *her* manager," Randy said, leaning his weight onto his forearms. "If you catch my drift."

"It's hard not to," Rod said cheerfully. "I'm downwind."

Harold snorted, then pretended to clear his throat, but Randy took no notice. "That's good," he said, apparently satisfied he'd made his point.

"Anyway," Rod continued, "the Club pays a fixed rate for all bands. Twelve hundred dollars."

Brenda's face lit up. "Sold!" she said, clapping her hands together. "When do you want us?"

"Let's figure on three or four dates this season. If it works out, we'll bring you back next year."

Brenda stretched her arms out to the side and let out a loud whoop. "This is great," she said.

Rod smiled. "Maybe with the extra bucks you can send your manager to night school. A couple of business courses might not hurt."

Randy puffed himself up in his chair. "Listen, pal, you better be careful what you say."

Rod leveled a bored look in his mirror's face. "Bud, I've just had three whiskey sours and a severe blow to the head. I'm liable to say anything." He turned to Brenda. "How about having dinner with me tomorrow night?"

Brenda laughed, but Randy gave her a hard look. "Babe, I want to know what the deal is with you and this guy."

"Just business, sweetie," she said, reaching across the table to pat the mermaid on his left arm. "I don't even know him."

"But she did kiss me the first time she saw me," Rod said. There was something building up in him now, a recklessness he hadn't felt since his rookie season on the tour. He'd been aggressive in those days, always hitting for the pin, always missing his putts on the high side of the cup. He didn't win much, but somehow that never seemed to matter.

"Sure, I told you about that," Brenda said quickly. "This is the guy I thought was you."

Randy looked Rod over carefully. "How the hell could you think that? This dork's not anything like me."

"I appreciate the thought," said Rod. He felt a meanness working its way out of him now.

Randy rocked his chair back and propped his boot against the table leg. "So how was it, sport? Was it a pretty hot kiss?" There was a dare in his tone Rod couldn't resist.

"It was great," Rod said. "I fell in love on the spot. I might even want to marry her." He smiled at Brenda, who seemed suddenly at a loss for something to say.

"Listen to this asshole," said Randy. "I ought to break his goddamn face."

"Play nice, Randy," Brenda said. The warning in her voice was for Rod's benefit, he knew. Underneath the table she curled her foot around his ankle. It was such a junior-high gesture Rod almost laughed out loud.

"You're perfect," he told her. "You're the woman I need." He stroked his fingers lightly across the back of her hand.

"That's it, buster," Randy said, rising from the table. "I want to see you outside."

Rod didn't know when he'd ever felt so happy. "Fine with me," he said. "I'll just pay the check and be right out."

Randy stormed away through the crowd. Rod watched him leave, then called a waitress over and ordered a bottle of champagne.

"What the hell do you think you're doing?" Harold asked him.

"Just playing the angles." He winked at Brenda. "We'll write up the contract when I come back."

"*If* you come back," she said, pouting. "Randy's a pretty tough guy. He gets in fights all the time."

"That just means he's stupid," Rod said, taking her by the hand. "Anyway, I've done some market research." She seemed confused, so he took advantage, leaning over and kissing her on the mouth. He was giddy with risk: they were on their way.

"This whole town's crazy," said Harold.

Rod got up from the table and started for the door. He knew the odds were good that Randy had run into the Bear and was already spitting out teeth on the pavement. That would simplify things. But nothing was certain in the world —maybe the Bear had gone home for the night, and now Randy was outside working himself up into a punk frenzy over a fickle, stoned angel he'd already lost.

No matter. Rod felt comfortable either way. Sure, the packaging could be deceptive—Harold was right about that. But even if two products looked almost the same, in the long run one of them always turned out to be Brand X. As Rod walked out smiling into the yellow night, he had a pretty good idea which was which.

‹ ‹ ‹

Skull Shots

When Shirley Davies walked into the pro shop Saturday morning, no one noticed the ten-pound bucket of wet concrete she carried with her. The shop was mobbed with golfers absorbed in pre-tournament rituals—buying gloves, caps, cleats, tees, putters. Some shook out new umbrellas and bright plastic rain suits, precautionary gear inspired by the week's heavy rains. Some milled along the clothing aisles pricing windbreakers and socks and knitted shirts. Some hovered by the coffee table munching doughnuts and arguing the merits of their favorite pros, their favorite courses, their favorite brands of woods and irons. The serious ones huddled in the corners plotting strategy for the opening round. A threesome by the counter debated the options in

golf-ball design: one-piece or wound construction? liquid or solid centers? straight or random dimples? Balata or Surlyn covers? ninety or one hundred compression? and how could anyone be sure? Jovial insults and fragments of raunchy stories swirled noisily overhead. A bevy of old men studied the current handicap charts to make sure they'd been allotted all the free strokes they deserved. Strangers shouldered aimlessly through the crowd looking for their partners, their golf bags, their score cards, their tee times. Shirley was adrift in a sea of goofy hats and rainbowed polyester pants. It was as if her husband, Lyle, had been multiplied a hundredfold. She shuddered at the thought.

Not that Lyle was a golfer; he'd barely mastered the basics of putt-putt. Her love of the game, not his, had led them to join the Club in the first place. He'd gone along only because it made sense as a financial tactic—his real estate business was drying up fast and the Club meant a new circle of contacts. She had finally recognized the seediness of Lyle's approach, a seediness she could now sense in every man in the room—something that went beyond the tackiness of their clownlike wardrobes. They were all cocooned in a sort of commercialized obliviousness, a cheap faith somehow tied to the price of tea in China, a willful ignorance that Shirley could no longer abide.

Even her infatuation with Rod was behind her now. As she watched him ringing up the sale for a sleeve of balls, grinning like the circus ringmaster he was, she wondered what had snared her in the first place. Maybe just the fact that he wasn't Lyle. Every Monday and Thursday afternoon for the past six weeks he'd worked with her on her game. She had a tendency to skull the ball, particularly with her low irons, and Rod had tried to help her get past it. "You've got to get under the ball," he kept telling her. "Don't be afraid to take a divot." But for some reason she just couldn't do it. Every time she started on a downswing, some reflex straightened up her spine. Shot after shot would rocket briefly along the ground and then die in a tangle of long grass. She didn't care, though. It didn't matter that she couldn't stop skulling her shots: the rest of her outlook soared. She hadn't been touched in twenty years by any men but Lyle and her doctor, neither of whom counted. Rod's casual intimacy—his resting his hand on her arm, or steadying her hips, or breathing over her shoulder as he guided her backswing—had opened up whole continents of possibility. Their contact always left her flushed and even thankful for the skull shots that kept her taking lessons.

Of course, for Rod there was nothing personal about it, she knew that. He was just doing his job, the way a window dresser might rearrange the limbs of a mannequin.

When Rod finally caught sight of her standing by the putter display, he smiled broadly and waved her over. He looked tired today, she thought, and there was a large red bruise in the center of his forehead. He'd probably walked into a door. Rod was a nice guy in some ways, but from what Shirley had seen, he was almost as oblivious to the world as Lyle. She threaded her way through the crowd and set the heavy tub of cement on the counter between them.

"You picked a bad day to hit shags," he said, nodding to the tub. "The driving range is pretty crowded right now."

Shirley nearly laughed in his face. Was he really stupid enough to think she was lugging around a bucket of range balls? "No problem," she told him.

"The tournament's turned the whole place into a madhouse," he said cheerfully. "But things'll clear out in about an hour. Meantime, think about your body turn." He mimed the pivot of a follow-through. "That's where the distance comes from."

"I don't think I'll be practicing any today."

"Oh, it's not too bad out there," he said. "The course has drained pretty well."

Shirley smiled. "Like a wound," she said, and Rod's own smile glazed over. "I guess you haven't found my seven iron yet."

"Uh, no, it hasn't turned up. But I've told Jimmy to keep an eye open." He glanced over toward the bag room, where Jimmy Wickerham was sitting on a stool in the doorway cleaning a set of clubs. "Hey, Jimmy!" he called. "Any sign of that lost seven iron?"

Jimmy looked up from his work. "What lost seven iron?"

Rod turned back to Shirley. "What was it, a *Nancy Lopez?*"

"No, a *Patty Berg*. I've had the set for twenty years."

Jimmy slowly shook his head. "It's not in the bag room, I can tell you that. Maybe somebody on the grounds crew picked it up, but I'd probably already know about it if they had."

Rod raised his palms in a gesture of helplessness. "Sorry," he said. "Sometimes things just disappear. Socks in the dryer —you know."

"Sure," she agreed. "Anything can disappear." She folded her arms across the top of the bucket and leaned over the counter. "How's the tournament look so far?"

Rod chuckled. "Great. I thought the weather might do us in this year, but we got a hell of a turnout. Which reminds me, you can tell your husband everyone'll be over for the clambake this afternoon, as planned."

"You'd better tell him yourself." She wouldn't see Lyle anytime soon, she was sure of that. Not unless he dropped dead and she had to identify the body.

"It was nice of you folks to host it this year," he went on. "A lot of people think the clambake is the best part of the whole Member-Guest weekend. It gives the wives a chance to mingle."

Shirley felt the hair on the back of her neck stand up. "There are other ways to get the wives involved," she said.

Rod leaned toward her and lowered his voice. "Let's don't open that can of worms now," he said.

"This whole place is a can of worms," she said.

"No argument there," he said, glancing around to see who might be listening. "Look, I'm on your side in this. Women should have been allowed in the tournament. But you know Glen Hanshaw—he's got a lot of set ideas, and the Board went along with him. There was nothing I could do."

A sunburned man with dark blotches on his burly neck and arms shoved his way up to the counter. "Gimme a dozen Top Flights there, pal." He smiled benignly at Shirley and hitched up his pants. "You the doughnut girl?" he asked. "We're runnin' low."

"No," Shirley told him, "I'm not the doughnut girl."

Rod rang up the golf balls and tossed in a handful of tees, no charge. As he closed the cash drawer, Glen L. Hanshaw and his son Harold pushed their way around Shirley and wedged themselves, shoulder to shoulder, against the counter.

"Rod, we need an arbitrator," Glen said. His raw-throated growl put Shirley on edge, though she knew he was trying to sound playful. "If a ball stops right on the line, is it in bounds or out?"

"That depends," Rod answered, rubbing the red lump on his forehead. "Is the line chalk or imaginary?"

Shirley reached between Harold and Glen for her bucket and stepped backward into the crowd, jostling the cluster of golfers behind her. There was barely room to turn around now—several more foursomes had drifted in from the snack bar and the men's locker room—and she began to feel claustrophobic. Hugging the concrete tightly to her breast, she wove her way toward the bag-room door.

Jimmy sat engrossed on his stool, meticulously scraping the dirt from the grooves of a Spaulding three wood with an ice pick, pausing now and then to spit on the face of the club. Shirley set her bucket on the floor and picked up the two wood he'd already finished. It was an old model—a customized Executive that probably dated to the early seventies—but it gleamed like new. She was impressed. Of all the people in the clubhouse right now, this kid might be the only one who really knew what he was doing.

"Jimmy," she said, edging sideways into the doorway, "I need a little help."

He buffed the head of the three wood with his shirttail and reached past her to slide the club gingerly back into its bag. "Sure, Mrs. Davies," he said. "But I swear I don't know anything about your seven iron."

"I need the keys to one of the carts," she said.

He drew the battered driver from the bag and studied it. "The keys are already in 'em," he said, etching the first flecks of dirt from the club face. "But we can't rent you a cart right now—they're all reserved for the tournament." He suddenly looked up from his work and stared at her. "Hey, is it true you almost drowned the other day?"

Shirley returned the two wood to the bag and smiled. "Yeah, it is. Where'd you hear about it?"

"Bev told me. Sometimes I help her out at the snack bar

—you know, when I'm not cleaning clubs or raking sand traps. She said you went in the pool Wednesday when we had all that rain, and she had to go in after you."

"I guess that's right," Shirley said, picking up her bucket. "She went in after me."

Jimmy shook his head. "Man, that's pretty heavy."

"A real eye-opener," Shirley agreed. She squeezed past Jimmy into the bag room, a dark cubicle stinking of earth and leather, then walked quickly out the back door of the clubhouse.

The carts were arranged along the macadam stretch behind the pro shop in a tidy phalanx—four across and more than a dozen deep—each cart with a pair of bags already strapped in place. The morning sun had just cleared the trees and flashed now off the polished heads of a hundred sets of irons. The still-wet fairways glistened in the distance. By noon the day would turn muggy as the August heat steamed away the past week's rain, but for now the air was crisp, comfortable as home, and Shirley felt glad she was here, glad she hadn't died in the pool on Wednesday, glad she had been reborn.

Rebirth was how she looked at it, nothing less. There had been a moment underwater when she knew she was done for; a moment when the panic passed away and left her with the calm recognition that for better or worse she was shedding her life. And just like that it slipped away from her—not life itself, but the burden of it, the clot of details that for so many years had dragged her down. It was a moment as much of relief as regret, and she suddenly understood she'd been heading toward this for a long, long time. But then came Bev's arm across her chest, the quick return to air, the choking back alive again. Alive, but not in the same old life: she'd left that on the bottom of the pool, and the newfound lightness of the world astounded her.

She walked over to a cart in the last row and set the bucket of concrete on the floorboard. She read the names on the scorecard clipped to the steering wheel: Todd Mumford and Hal Sykes. Todd was one of the owners—with his brother Teddy—of the insurance agency Lyle had hooked them up with for their homeowner's policy. Todd smiled more than Teddy, which she supposed meant he was the better salesman of the two, though Shirley considered them both to be crooked. When she'd reported the leak in her foundation neither brother had been willing to do anything about it, so her basement still filled with water every time it rained. Hal Sykes was the Methodist minister who'd joined the Club early in the spring. Shirley had played nine holes with Hal and his wife, Eileen, one Sunday afternoon and had found them both to be about as bland as she'd expected. The only thing she had against Hal was that he was a terrible golfer, excruciatingly slow, who always picked up his ball after two or three bad shots so he never had a score to mark down. He certainly had no business playing in a tournament.

She unstrapped Todd's and Hal's bags and laid them in the

long brown puddle that skirted the low side of the macadam. As she climbed into the cart and shifted it to reverse, she heard someone call her name. It was Hal, hurrying over from the putting green.

"Shirley, wait," he called, a grin filling his face as if some comical mistake had been made. When he got close enough to see where Shirley had dumped his bag, he stopped grinning. "Hey, what do you think you're doing?"

Shirley eased the cart backward until she was clear of the formation, then stopped and shifted into forward.

"What are you doing?" he asked again.

Shirley looked at him and smiled. "Hal, I've been thinking about baptisms," she said.

Hal trotted over to his bag and lifted it from the water, careful not to let the runoff drain too near his wing tips. "Look at this!" he said, touching his fingers to the soggy white yarn of his head covers, all four of which were now streaked with brown.

"Here's the way I see it," Shirley went on. "When John the Baptist dunked all those people in the Jordan, it wasn't a ritual, it was a no-holds-barred wrestling match."

"Look at this," Hal said again, pulling off the head covers and dangling them at arm's length like dead fish. "Eileen gave me these for Father's Day."

"She must be a wonderful woman," said Shirley, and she drove out onto the course.

The opening foursome was just teeing off when she cut

across the first fairway in front of them. They yelled something to her, but the sputter of the cart drowned out their words. She guessed they were telling her to keep off the fairways—carts were supposed to stay in the rough after heavy rains so the spinning tires wouldn't scuff up the good grass. She swerved into the long, wet rough, sending a spray up behind her, and headed toward the far side of the course, to the fifth green, where no one from the clubhouse could see her.

She parked the cart between the green and a sand trap and lifted the bucket of concrete onto the seat beside her. It occurred to her that she'd forgotten to bring a trowel, but she decided her hands would do just as well. She peeled up the rubbery plastic lid and flung it away behind her. That gave her a good feeling, and she giggled. She couldn't remember ever doing a thing like that before—throwing something away without watching to see where it landed. It was something Lyle could never do.

She carried the bucket across the spongy green and set it by the pin. The flag flopped lazily in the breeze. Shirley lifted the red metal staff from the hole and chucked it like a javelin out into the fairway. It stuck for a moment in the soft ground, then fell with a slight rattle onto the grass. She dipped her fingers into the doughy concrete and scooped out a cool, moist handful. Evening out the pebbly grit with her palms, she worked the concrete slowly into a ball and pressed it firmly into the empty cup. The hole was still half empty, so she scooped up a second, larger handful and packed it in over the first. When she'd smoothed the small mound to ground level, she stuck a long fingernail into the damp surface and traced a delicate "S" across the top.

As she climbed back into the cart and started toward the fourth green, she found herself thinking about Lyle again. Nothing specific—what haunted her now was Lyle in his purest form, Lyle the presence, Lyle the idea. He stretched like a canvas across the back of her mind, and no matter which way she pointed her thoughts he was right there, just over her shoulder, filling in the landscape and tampering with the view. Whatever passed before her in the world she saw through both their eyes, and it was his dim vision she struggled with at every fork in the road.

It was her own fault, this infection—she knew that. She'd stayed with Lyle twenty years too long, and now every pathway in her brain was cluttered with his belongings. She would always know which foods he liked, which television shows, which brand of aspirin. There would never be a way to leave all that behind; her past with him would be perpetual, a constant face in the mirror, a weathering she would carry with her like chicken pox scars, creeping arthritis, and reknitted bones. The very dust of him would stay lodged in her lungs forever.

She cemented the fourth, third, and sixth holes without being seen, since all of those greens were on the back side of the course. The second hole was in plain view of the front porch of the pro shop, so she decided to cut across to the seventh, an elevated par three nestled in a grove of trees. As she rounded the rain shelter by the seventh tee, she turned to look back over her shoulder toward the clubhouse to make sure she was still hidden from view. It didn't occur to her that she should keep her eyes on the path ahead in case someone had rearranged the scenery. She didn't even know what she'd hit until after the cart had banged noisily to a halt.

"Christ Almighty! Look where you're going!"

Shirley felt a wave of tiny burstings in her brain as the adrenaline flashed through her. In half a second it was gone, like a skyrocket spending itself in a shower of sparks, but the impact left her shaking. So—she could still be frightened, after all. That was good to know. It meant her reflexes were sound, that certain parts of her remained undamaged.

But what had she done now? She looked around at the mess in front of her: pieces of plastic and aluminum tubing lay scattered through the wet grass, along with several sheets of crumpled posterboard, some loose golf balls, and a pair of air conditioners. Standing between the air conditioners with his arms spread wide and his mouth hanging open was Ed Betzger, of Ed Betzger's Heating and Cooling Supply.

Ed pointed forlornly to her front tire. "You wrecked my display," he said. Shirley peered over the dashboard. Two legs of a card table jutted from beneath her cart like a pair of tusks.

"Sorry," she said. "I wasn't expecting anybody to be here."

"You wrecked it," he said again, and Shirley wondered why it was that men she talked to tended so often to repeat themselves. Did she look like someone who didn't hear things the first time? "It's all wrecked," Ed went on, picking up a sheet of posterboard that had been carefully lettered with a red felt-tip marker. "Win a 5,000-BTU Air Conditioner for a Hole in One!" it read. He tried to shake the water from the sign, but that only made the letters bleed across the cardboard. Finally he dropped the sheet back into the wet grass and wiped his hands on his pants. "I'm not covered for this kind of thing," he said.

Shirley shifted into reverse and tried to ease back off the card table, but one of the legs snagged on the undercarriage. Before Ed could stop her she floored the accelerator, dragging the table backward until it caught on an uneven piece of ground. Then, with a pop and crunch, the table seemed to leap from under the front of the cart. Ed rushed forward and bent over it like he was examining a roadkill, touching a hand gently to one of the mangled legs. From the cart Shirley could see the ragged crack that ran the length of the pressboard top.

"Looks like a goner," she said.

Ed stood up and looked at her. "Mrs. Davies, I'm afraid I'm gonna have to charge you for the damages," he said. He nodded to the air conditioners. "Those are brand-new units."

"They look all right to me," she said.

Ed tipped one of the air conditioners upright and plucked a few clumps of muddy grass from the vents. "This facing is cracked," he said.

"That ought to be easy enough to replace," she suggested.

Ed shook his head and walked over to her cart. "Look, Mrs. Davies, both of these units are banged up now. I'd never be able to get full price. I mean, if you hit an air conditioner with a golf cart, it's just not new anymore."

Shirley couldn't imagine why Bev Musselman had ever gone to bed with this guy. Didn't she have any standards at all? Or maybe it wasn't true—maybe the whole story about Bev's sneaking up to the stockroom with Ed Betzger was nothing but gossip. After all, she'd only heard it from Lyle, and he wouldn't know the truth if it fell on him from an airplane.

Ed smoothed his shirtfront over his belly. "I'll tell you what—I've got to go over to your place tomorrow anyway to pick up those coolers your husband rented for the clambake. Him and me'll work something out." He broke into a broad smile, and Shirley could see that Ed had finally realized what a windfall this accident could be. Apparently she wasn't the only one who knew her husband was a sap.

Ed seemed about to say something else, but his attention suddenly focused on her steering wheel. "What happened to your hands?" he asked.

Shirley released her grip and held her fingers up in front of her. The concrete had dried to a crusty white residue, leaving both her hands looking like the diseased remains of an unwrapped mummy.

"I recently died," she told him.

Ed chuckled and drew a fat cigar from his shirt pocket. "You and me both," he said. "What was it killed you off?"

Shirley rubbed her hands together, flaking off a shower of scales. "Nothing I didn't see coming." She blew across her knuckles and a puff of white powder rose in the air.

Ed propped a foot on the bumper rail and lit his cigar. "Yeah, I guess that's what kills everybody off," he said. "Take air conditioners, for instance—" He tossed his burned match toward the two damaged units. "The freon in those things'll probably get us all. Every time we crank one up, it sucks a little more life out of the planet. We know it, but we just keep right on."

"So why don't you stop selling them?"

He shrugged. "People haven't stopped buying them."

"Maybe you'd see things differently if you had kids."

"Oh, I've got kids," he said. "A boy and a girl. They live with their mother out in Oklahoma. My girl's getting married next month."

Shirley sat silent on the vinyl cushion. The soft sputter of distant golf carts drifted over from the second fairway. The almost empty bucket lay overturned on the floorboard beside her. There was enough concrete left to fill one or two more holes, but suddenly she didn't see the point. Even if she plugged them all, the tournament would still turn out the same. In a few minutes the first group would find out what she'd done. They'd be baffled at first. Someone would go back to the clubhouse to tell Rod, who would then call Artie, the greenskeeper. Artie would send a crew out with hole diggers to relocate the cups. Meanwhile, foursome after foursome would stall on the third tee, waiting for the greens to open up, and Shirley would be their single topic of conversation. She would become the clown of the tournament, the loony they would all joke about at the dinner-dance on Sunday night. They'd probably talk about her next year, too, and the year after that. Was this what she had wanted—to be the cornerstone of some comic myth golfers laughed about between shots?

No. She wanted something else, though she wasn't sure what to call it. She wanted her seven iron back in her bag. She wanted her golf lessons to make some difference in her game. She wanted a tee time on Saturday morning, when women weren't supposed to play. She wanted a clear ruling: if the ball stops right on the line, is it in bounds or out?

She wanted to know why she had poured twenty years of her life into a gaping hole.

Why in God's name did people get married? No, she

knew the cruel answer to that: postcards of sunny skies, the season warm enough to go naked. But why did so many of them stay married for so long, even after the weather had turned and the chill had set in. Couldn't all those newlyweds at Niagara Falls look up at the water tumbling endlessly over the edge and sense what kind of life they might expect? Didn't they know a honeymoon was never real, that it was just a sad time-out, that someday there would be nothing left of the trip but the baggage?

She didn't understand any of it. Ed Betzger had children in Oklahoma, and she had a set of golf clubs. Was that really how life parceled itself out? Air conditioners leached away the atmosphere, and her shag balls were cut full of smiles from skull shots she couldn't stop making. Her hands were gloved in concrete, like fossils waiting for the next ten million years.

She shifted the cart into forward again and turned it toward the clubhouse. "Sorry about all this," she said.

Ed flicked the first ash from his cigar and gazed around at the demolished display. "How about a lift back to the clubhouse?" he said. "Maybe they've got a table I can borrow."

"Sure," Shirley said. "Climb in."

Ed settled himself stiffly on the seat beside her. "You know, I've never ridden in a golf cart before," he said, smiling.

Shirley smiled, too. The drive back would be pleasant. She could stick to the path this time, and meander with it down past the stables and the lake. She could point things out to Ed along the way: "That's where I had my first birdie," and "Once I broke a four wood on that tree." Then when they reached the clubhouse, she would say goodbye to Ed and get her putter from the bag room. If she passed Rod in the pro shop, she might pinch his side and playfully muss his curly hair. She would shout hellos across the veranda to members she had met before, then join the throng of golfers on the practice green. She would introduce herself to strangers and urge them to call her by her name. She would touch them warmly on the arm and compliment them on their outfits. Maybe she would tell them things about herself, about her life with Lyle, about how disappointed she was in the way it had all turned out. Maybe she would even tell some suntanned dreamboat he could have her for a song. Why not? She was down to her last half hour of friendly faces; it would be a shame to waste it.

‹ ‹ ‹

Mule Collector

The new mule pushed his way in among the others and pressed his muzzle tentatively against the sparkling walls of Glen L. Hanshaw's glassed-in patio. Glen L. stood for a moment in the kitchen doorway, iced tea in hand, admiring the scene around him. All six of his mules were out there, spaced irregularly around the patio's three exposed sides, running their lips and tongues along the sticky surface, sometimes clacking their big teeth against the shatter-resistant glass. Even through the smeared slobber that partly clouded his view, he could see the inner workings of the mouths, the jaws moving in a chorus of silent conversation, telling him things that only mules could know.

He moved methodically across the flagstone floor and

eased himself into the webbing of his lounge chair, careful not to spill too much of his tea. He'd overextended himself today, first on the golf course and then with the mules, and now even the mild strain of steadying his full glass brought tremors from some fault line in his legs or back or brain. He set the tea on the floor beside him and closed his eyes to rest.

The tournament had taken more out of him than he'd expected. He'd ridden in a cart, of course, but even so a full nine holes was more than he was used to these days. He'd fallen into the habit of playing only abbreviated rounds— starting at the fourth hole, which ran parallel to his mule field, and finishing on the seventh green, just across the fairway from his house. Maybe a two-day tournament was more than he could handle. Already he felt the muscles along the backs of his legs and arms stiffening like old leather, and the thought of having to play another full round tomorrow gave him a sudden chill.

Or was that the air conditioning? The blistering heat on the course today had baked him like a clay pot, so as soon as he'd made it back to the house, even before tending to the mules, he'd cranked the thermostat up into the blue arctic range. Now goose bumps rose from his raw patches of sunburn. That was all right, though. He enjoyed being uncomfortably cold on the hottest day of the year. That's what being rich was all about.

For their part, the mules seemed perfectly content, the half dozen of them ranged in the long shade of the house, pressing their gums against the cool, sweet glass. They knew how to tolerate the heat, how to pace themselves against the mercury, moving only when they had a better place to go. Glen L. hadn't understood that as a boy. He remembered walking the plow behind his father's big pair of drays, breaking sod for a late-summer crop. On hot days the mules worked more slowly, keeping him longer in the fields, and he had hated them for that. But now he understood their stubbornness: a bad sun called for a slower pace, plain and simple. Why hadn't he known that back then?

"Hey, Dad! Are you home?" The voice startled him, and Glen L. suddenly remembered that he wasn't alone in the house this weekend. One of his sons had come to visit, and they were partners in the Member-Guest. But what the hell was his name?

"I'm out here," Glen L. called. "On the patio."

"I got us a couple of steaks, and all the fixings," the boy announced from the kitchen. Glen L. heard the papery rattle of grocery sacks being dumped on the counter.

Harold, that was it: the boy's name was Harold. Bill was the one who was dead.

"I thought you'd be going to the tournament clambake," Glen L. called. "It's already paid for."

"I'm not much on clams," Harold said. He stepped out onto the patio. "I thought maybe we'd get out the grill . . ."

Glen L. looked up at his son: not a boy anymore, but a

fat, bald fifty-year-old with broken blood vessels mapping his cheeks and nose, his mouth now hanging open like a clubbed fish. But Harold wasn't a fish. He was something more lamentable, more obsolete. A 1966 Corvair, that was it: he was a 1966 Corvair barreling flat out for the scrap heap. But how could that be? How could a son of his be such an old man already? And where did that leave Glen L.?

"Jesus Christ," Harold muttered. "What the hell's going on out here?"

"I'm watching my mules."

"But, I mean"—he gestured toward the smeared walls—"what the hell are they doing?"

"They're licking the glass," Glen L. told him. He pointed to the small plastic bucket and broad-bristled paintbrush stationed by the patio door. "I coat the walls with wet sugar every afternoon. It's their special treat."

Harold sat down heavily in the BarcaLounger. "But it's grotesque." He scanned the row of mules uneasily, his blue eyes bright and watery like his mother's.

"The mules seem to like it," Glen L. said, reaching down for his tea. "Especially the new one. I think the group activity helps him fit in."

"New one?" Harold scowled through a quick head count, then shook his head. "Christ, Dad, you can't keep doing this."

Glen L. smiled. "I found an old sugar mule over in Able

County. Got a great deal. Sugar mules are pretty rare around here. The farmer didn't even know what he had—thought it was a *cotton* mule. Can you imagine that?"

Harold sighed and reached over to steady the heavy cut-crystal glass in his father's hand. "Here, let me help you," he said, lifting it away, and Glen L. realized he'd sloshed some tea across the front of his shirt. He wiped at it clumsily with his fingers, pressing the cold spill against his stomach. When he looked up, Harold was standing by him with a roll of paper towels.

"Now I'm in the market for a couple of good pack mules," he said, dabbing a wad of towels along the stain. "But this is the wrong part of the country, so I might have to wait a while."

Harold cleared his throat and stared at the mule directly in front of him, a male Missouri with crooked, blackened teeth. "Six mules is a pretty big responsibility."

Glen L. snorted. "Six? Six is nothing. You know what my inventory is down at the car lot? I can show you sixty brand-new Cadillacs any goddamn day of the year."

"I know, Dad. But running the dealership isn't the same thing as filling up your yard with mules. I don't think you can equate the two."

Glen L. felt a flare of anger. What the hell way was that for a son to talk to his father? *I don't think you can equate the two.* Like some schoolteacher talking to a backward kid. If

Glen L. had ever said anything like that to his own father, he'd have felt a leather strap across his backside. "I can equate anything I want," he said, though he knew that was a lie.

He could never equate Harold and Bill, for example. Bill had been a born salesman, like his father, and could have done anything—run his own company, maybe, or had his own TV show, or even gone into politics. But Harold had become—what was it again?—some kind of accountant. An actuarial accountant, that was it, working in a sunless office up at the state capital. Gray rooms and long numbers and cold marble floors. True, Glen L. had never actually seen the place; but he'd been there in his mind, and it felt just like a morgue.

Harold stepped over to the glass wall and drummed his fingers lightly above the Missouri mule's head, but the animal didn't seem to notice.

"Don't get them started," Glen L. warned.

Harold stopped tapping the glass. "What do you mean?"

"I mean they're quiet now, but if you spook one he'll start to bray. And if one starts, the others are liable to join in. That'll make one hell of a racket." He smiled at the thought. The truth was, he loved it when his mules got rowdy. Of course, from time to time a few upstarts from the Country Club complained about the noise, but that didn't worry him. It was his Club, after all. He'd helped found it back in

'48, and had written most of the bylaws himself. For the last twenty years he'd even been Club president. Let the new members grouse all they wanted—he knew the Board would never dare take him on.

"Sorta like a zoo, isn't it?" Glen L. said. "Except we're the ones inside. That makes it better, I think."

"Sure," said Harold, but from the way he chewed his lower lip Glen L. could see he wasn't sure at all. Lip chewing was a giveaway Harold had inherited from his mother—a skittish woman, really, overly polite, who almost never spoke her mind. For thirty-eight years she'd kept her conversations with Glen L. on a sort of cruise control set below the speed limit, and he had learned to look for meanings in her face, rather than her words. "How are you feeling?" he would ask, and she'd always say, "Fine," even in the end, when her body made it clear she was dying.

Glen L. reached again for his glass of tea, and with a concentrated effort, lifted it smoothly to the armrest of his chair. "Remember the time I took you boys to the Washington zoo?" he asked. "Nineteen fifty-six. We saw the real Smokey the Bear. I bet you forgot about that."

Harold smiled. "No, I remember," he said, easing himself back into the BarcaLounger. "We fed him a bag of peanuts."

"That's right. You boys fed peanuts to Smokey the Bear. That's something to be proud of. It's like being part of American history."

"Well, I guess . . ."

"Then we went to Mount Vernon. Drove out there in the snow. Had just about the whole damn place to ourselves."

"And froze our butts off," Harold said.

Glen L. frowned and waved the notion away as if it were a puff of smoke. "That part doesn't matter." He leaned over sideways and took a careful sip of tea. "You know, this instant mix is pretty good stuff. It's got the sugar and the lemon already in it. You don't have to do a thing but add water."

"Uh, yeah, I think I've had it before."

"The thing I hate about regular iced tea is you can't ever get the sweetness right. No matter how hard you stir, the sugar won't ever dissolve, it just swirls around a while and then sinks to the bottom." He lifted the glass briefly between them. "But this stuff is great," he said, and for a long moment they both stared at the sweating half-glass of tea, almost as if they expected it to do something.

"Maybe I'll have some later," Harold said finally.

Glen L. suddenly remembered why he'd brought up Mount Vernon. "George Washington was the first commercial mule breeder in America," he announced. "I bet you didn't know that."

Harold looked at him suspiciously. "I didn't think you could breed mules," he said. "I thought mules were all sterile."

Glen L. shook his head. "Christ, Harold, did you just fall

off the turnip truck? What I mean is he imported jackasses to crossbreed with his mares." He sighed and wiped the back of his wrist across his lips. "Anyway, only the males are guaranteed sterile. Your grandfather had a female hinny once that turned out to be fertile." He paused. "But I guess you don't even know what a hinny is."

Harold shrugged. "Some kind of mule, I guess."

A slow smile smoothed the wrinkles from Glen L.'s lips. "It's exactly like a mule. In fact, you probably couldn't tell the difference in a million years. But," he said, widening his eyes to emphasize the mystery, "it's not really a mule at all. Not in the least." He settled his head back against the chair webbing, satisfied that he'd just given Harold the clue he needed to make his way properly through life.

Harold didn't notice. "You seem to know a lot about mules," he said.

"More than I ever knew about cars." Harold wouldn't believe him, of course, but it was true. After forty years of owning the local Cadillac franchise, he still couldn't explain the difference between one car and another. Oh, he could sell them all right—but that didn't mean much. He supposed that was the secret most salesmen lived with—that the talent to sell was a thing in itself and could live, even thrive, with no real connection to the product. In Glen L.'s case, he had memorized the options lists and the names of all the technical features that complicated each new model's engine, but rarely had he comprehended even the simplest mechanical workings behind the words. In his own driving, the most basic forms of car maintenance had remained alien to him—things other people might consider routine, like changing an oil filter, or tightening a fan belt, or replacing a wiper blade. In fact, it had always been a point of pride with him that whenever the slightest thing went wrong with whatever car he was driving, he'd just turn it over to his mechanics and pick another demo from his endless stock of cars. And he never used the self-serve pumps.

But mules were something he had studied all his life—or at least it seemed that way to him now.

"Pretty soon you won't see any mules at all except in zoos," Glen L. said, pushing himself up from his chair. "There's just no call for them anymore. It's all tractors now."

Harold rose quickly and steadied his father by the elbow, then caught the glass of tea as it slid from the aluminum armrest. Glen L. looked at the rescued drink in Harold's hand, then up at his son's sad eyes, and felt things going wrong inside. The stepstones in his mind seemed suddenly too far apart, and he couldn't make the leaps. "Too fast," he said, meaning he had stood up quicker than he should and had been swamped in a blood rush of dizziness. This had happened to him frequently, he knew that much. Brief spells of confusion, always worse when he was tired. Hardening of the arteries, that's what they used to call it when a mind slowed down enough to lose its way. These days they proba-

bly had a dozen different labels for troubles in the brain—
names as specific as Oldsmobile and Chrysler, each with its
own set of options. In the end, he imagined, they were all
more or less interchangeable. Besides, it hardly mattered
what name his problems went by—medical terms were just
as meaningless to him as the numbers on an engine.

"That's progress, I guess," said Harold, offering a weak
smile, and Glen L. saw that whatever he'd just said to his son
must have been misunderstood. He tried to speak again,
concentrating hard to keep the words from turning into
strangers, from unforming themselves on the tip of his
tongue and stalling him in silence. But the dizziness came
again like a cool, damp cloth behind his eyes, wiping his
thoughts clean. He cleared his throat and tried again, certain
he had to say something, even if it made no sense. Awkward
pauses made customers uneasy, and that was bad for business.

"What is it you're here for?" he heard himself asking.
What is it you're here for? Glen L. turned the sound of it over
in his mind. Yes, it was a good, sincere question. He knew
Harold had come to stay with him for a couple of days, but
the reason had momentarily escaped him. Asking about it
seemed only logical, a simple step to steady him with a frame
of reference. But Harold only blinked and turned his gaze
toward the floor. It was his guilty look, and even though
Glen L. couldn't immediately sort out the language to say so,
he could see that the boy felt stung, as if the question had
gone deeper than he'd intended.

"Let's talk about it later," Harold said.

"No such thing," Glen L. snapped. Hadn't this boy learned anything from his old man's four decades in sales? There was no later: later was a sham, a sidestep, a customer's excuse, a pitch gone wrong. It meant no deal, no dice, no chance in hell.

"I just thought it might be better to talk some other time." Harold waved a chubby finger toward the line of mules. "You know—when there aren't so many distractions. What I want to say is kinda serious."

"Everything's serious," Glen L. said. "Rebates, dealer prep, destination charges, factory incentives. Everything." He wasn't sure that was quite what he'd meant to say, but it was close enough.

Harold raised his head and looked steadily at his father. Glen L. tried to meet his gaze, but suddenly shivered, recalling an expression in his own father's eyes, that same look of —what? What was it he saw there? Weariness? Disappointment? Or maybe something else, something Glen L. couldn't remember the word for. Maybe there was no word. But it was a dark look, and it had always made him feel small and troublesome, a boy who somehow didn't measure up. What right did Harold have to wear that look? It wasn't a son's look at all.

"Well, I'm just a little worried, is all," Harold said.

Glen L. nodded. "My mules," he said, and stepped away from his chair to the streaked patio wall. The animals had finished licking away the sugar coating, and stood now staring sleepily ahead into the cool blue tint of the glass. Beyond the mules, Glen L. could see a late foursome trudging up the fourth fairway through the now broken afternoon heat, and he felt a wave of contentment. He loved living by the Country Club. It gave him a view greener than his own father's farm. So quiet and picturesque—like a postcard of some foreign land.

Emily had been happy enough here, he felt sure of that. Happy as she could have been, anyway. Some people were born to be alcoholics and some people weren't, that was the way Glen L. saw it. Maybe it was genetics or maybe it was some other stroke of fate, but whatever the case, there was nothing anybody could do about it. There was certainly nothing Glen L. could have done about it. Emily had just been one of the unlucky ones. That wasn't Glen L.'s fault.

It wasn't even Bill's fault, though that would be an easy place to put the blame, with his killing himself like that. Killing himself. That was the one thing Emily never could get past. Of course, Bill hadn't done it on purpose. He'd slipped, that was all. Glen L. was sure of that. All kids played on water towers, and sometimes accidents happened. There was no reason in the world for Bill to have jumped.

And the boys, too, they'd loved living here and having the room to romp as far and wild as they pleased. The yard had been unfenced in those days—no mules to keep in. Though there might have been a dog.

"It's not only the mules, Dad. I'm just not sure you can keep on living by yourself like this. You're not—well, you're not as sharp as you used to be. You need somebody to look after you."

Harold stopped talking then, and in the space that opened between them, Glen L. gradually assembled Harold's meaning. It crystallized slowly, like a ball of ice, growing clear and hard in his mind. The more he thought, the more he understood; and the more he understood, the colder he got. Harold wanted him put away, that was the gist of it. After all he had done for this boy, Harold wanted him hauled off to the dump like some rusted-out junker. Well, by God he wouldn't have it. Glen L. had never needed anybody, his family included, and he'd be damned if he'd let a son of his tell him what to do with his life. Maybe Emily would've put up with that kind of disrespect, letting her precious boys say and do whatever the hell they wanted—but not him. No, by God, no son could talk like that and get away with it—that was the one thing he'd learned from his own father. He'd teach this boy who ought to be put away. He'd whip the son of a bitch until he bled. Glen L. could still do that, he still had the right. He'd show this little shit which one of them was boss.

He groped along the top of his trousers for his belt, but couldn't find it. Someone had taken it from him, and he hadn't even noticed. What the hell was happening to him? He began to panic.

"What is it, Dad?" Harold asked, putting his hand lightly on the side of Glen L.'s arm. Glen L. flinched at the touch. Snake. Harold was a goddamn snake. "What's wrong?"

"Need my belt," Glen L. stammered. "Need—" He patted desperately at his stomach and hips, but it was no use. His belt was gone, and his words were failing. He couldn't argue, and he couldn't punish. The rage rose up in him, huge and spiteful, but found nowhere to go. A gulping sob broke from his throat, and he closed his eyes tight, fighting for control.

"It's all right," Harold told him. "You didn't wear a belt today. These pants have an elastic waist, see?" Harold hooked a finger in the top of Glen L.'s pants and tugged. The waistline stretched like a rubber band, then snapped back smartly into place.

As Glen L. stared down at the front of his plaid elastic pants, he felt the blood surging in his head, and the instant he felt it, he knew that his thoughts were scattering again, that some unfathomable tide had swept over him, dragging his mind away from whatever he'd been struggling with. His anger, unmoored from its source, flaked apart like old sheet metal, and he felt suddenly calm again, pleasantly light-headed, with no particular need to sort through the fragments that remained. He had asked a question about his belt, he remembered, and Harold had answered him: Glen L. had no belt, and it was all right. Why had he worried about his belt? he wondered. It had something to do with Harold—

Harold had said something wrong. But what did the belt have to do with it? Maybe Harold had teased him about his pants. That was probably it—they really were pretty silly-looking off the golf course. Well, no matter. No harm done. Harold was always putting his foot in his mouth. He never had the gift of gab like his brother Bill. That Bill was a born salesman. Poor Harold couldn't make a pitch if his life depended on it. But they were both good boys.

Funny that he couldn't call to mind how Bill had died. It might have had something to do with cars—an accident of some kind. But maybe not; maybe he was only mixing up different parts of his life. Anyway, it would come to him sooner or later. The important things always drifted back, sometimes even after he'd stopped expecting them.

Looking out across the golf course now, he remembered why Harold had come home to visit. They were partners in the Member-Guest, just like last year and the year before. Just like every year since the tournament began. They'd actually won it a couple of times, back in their salad days. Harold had once been a pretty fair golfer, he had to admit. Better even than Bill.

"These tournaments are rough on an old man," he said cheerily. "How about you pick us up some steaks, and we'll bring out the grill tonight."

"Sounds pretty good," Harold told him.

"Did you get a chance to check the leader board before you left the Club?"

"Yeah, I checked it."

"How're we doing?"

"We're doing fine, Dad."

"Within striking distance?"

"Absolutely."

"Well, don't stay out too late tonight. Tomorrow we'll make our move."

The shadows were lengthening now, and Harold switched on the floor lamp by the patio table. A shiver of movement passed among the mules, and as Glen L. turned again to watch them, he saw his own faint outline hovering in the glass. Then his eyes focused on the gently swaying mules, and for a moment he forgot why they were there.

This wasn't the view he'd expected his life to come to. He'd expected to pass out his days sitting on the patio with Emily, the two of them watching their grandkids tear across the neatly trimmed lawn. He'd even imagined putting in a pool for days like this. But now he was an old man with brittle bones, and the lawn was a ruin, cut to pieces by the sharp trampling of hooves. There was no pool, there were no grandkids, there was no Bill, there was no Emily. Harold was his only remnant. He might as well have been a mule himself, for all he'd leave behind him in the world.

Glen L. took his iced tea from Harold's hand and gulped down the last few sugary swallows. His dizziness had passed for now, and he felt clearheaded, more like his old self. But the spells weren't over, he knew that. If anything, they'd come more often now, stealing treasures from his mind like so many pickpockets, each theft so smooth he might not ever know what he had lost.

Was that a good thing, or a bad?

He looked at Harold, who stood in the kitchen doorway now with his fingers laced beneath his belly as if he were holding himself up. "You need to take better care of yourself, Harold," he said. "You look like death on a shingle." Harold smiled, almost like a boy again, and for a moment Glen L. felt younger, too. "Let's kick up our heels," he said, and before Harold could even ask what he meant, Glen L. turned toward the mules and banged the heavy iced-tea glass sharply against the patio wall, rattling the panel in its frame. The new sugar mule jerked its head violently to the side, knocking the bad-tempered Missouri in the teeth. The startled Missouri let out a bray and shoved itself sideways against the line of mules to give itself more room to fight. The still-panicked sugar mule drew its head upright and tried to retreat from the wall, but stepped into the fetlock of the dray on its other side. The dray nipped the sugar mule viciously on the shoulder, and now all three mules began to slam back and forth against the line. In a matter of moments nearly all the mules were stumbling sideways in confusion, stepping all over one another, snapping and kicking, braying angrily at the disruption in their lives.

Glen L. leaned forward against the cool plate glass. It was a thrilling spectacle, better than Mount Vernon or the Washington zoo, better than anything he could ever remember seeing. "It's like a piece of American history," he said happily as his son pulled him back from the glass.

They were all singing now, all six of them, and they'd never been in finer form. Their clamor echoed through the porch, raw-edged and harsh, but still oddly tuneful, a sassy chorus crowding out the air. It was the most complicated sound Glen L. could imagine—far more complicated than the chugging of an engine; more complicated even than salvaging lost words.

In some ways it was ugly, like a hopeless pain worming between the ribs.

But that wasn't all of it, not by a long shot. It was a good sound, too—solid and strong, with a wild streak flashing crazily through its heart. If he closed his eyes and listened without thinking, it lodged in his bones like something native, something inborn, something older than his father's oldest mule.

In those ways, it sounded like laughter.

‹ ‹ ‹

Steamed Clams

If Brenda had known that Rod's idea of a dinner date was to stand around in some stranger's back yard with a bunch of golfers eating steamed clams, she'd have told him to find some other decoration to hang on his arm. But she hadn't thought to ask, and he hadn't sprung it on her until they were already in the car. So here she was, overdressed in spike heels and fake pearls, trying to collect herself before Rod ushered her up the driveway. She needed a drink.

She needed six drinks. Crowds always made her uncomfortable, and even though she knew that these golfers and their wives were a pretty harmless bunch compared to what she was used to down at the tavern, she didn't like the idea of there being so many of them. Any mob could turn

nasty; she'd at least learned that much singing with the band.

Just last week at a five-hundred-dollar bar gig, some drunk had hit their synthesizer with a squeeze bottle of ketchup. Randy had come along that night to hustle some pool, and when the trouble started he dove right in and beat a guy senseless. Not the guy who threw the ketchup, it turned out. But that didn't matter to Randy.

"Are you sure this is the right house?" she asked, though she knew it was. There were Cadillacs and Lincolns parked up and down the block.

Rod checked the piece of paper with the Davieses' address and reread the numbers above the front door. "It must be," he said. "But you're right—I had no idea the place would be so run-down."

Run-down? What was run-down about it? The shingles were still on the roof and none of the windows were broken. The porch looked level. There weren't any tires in the yard, and the grass was mowed. God, if he thought this was run-down, what would he think when he saw her place?

"What's that?" she asked, pointing at what seemed to be an arrow sticking from the wall between the windows on the upper story. Rod squinted up at the feathered shaft.

"I'm not sure what that is," he said. "Maybe some kind of sundial. I've seen them mounted on houses before."

"I think I'm out of my element here."

He took her by the hand and pulled her gently forward.

"Relax," he said. "These people are about as innocuous as they come."

Innocuous? What would Randy say to a word like that?

A cluster of old men at the far end of the driveway suddenly caught sight of them and called out a chorus of hellos. Rod waved back, smiling tightly.

"I don't like being the only outsider," she told him.

"You're not," he said, keeping his grin trained on the crowd. "Most of these folks barely know each other. This party's for the Member-Guest tournament—half the people here are guests."

"They all look like members to me," she said, taking in the sea of wizened faces. "Anyway, I won't know anybody."

"You know Harold Hanshaw—he might be here. He's in the tournament with his father."

"I don't know Harold Hanshaw."

"Sure you do. He was at our table last night. I introduced you."

"Meeting a guy once doesn't mean I know him," Brenda said, though it wasn't a point she wanted to stress. After all, she didn't know Rod any better than she knew Harold Hanshaw. "And there's no music. How can you call it a party when there's no music?"

"We'll just stay for a little while," he promised. "I always have to show up for these things, but I don't have to stay too long."

Always? Is this what dating a golf pro would be like? Even

Randy plugged her into a more appealing crowd than this, and his friends were all criminals and speed freaks. If this was the best Rod could do, she'd have to cut him loose in a hurry.

Well, not a big hurry. Rod was a cute guy, even exciting in a sort of square-cornered way. And for God knew what reason, he seemed genuinely crazy about her, crazy enough to ask her out in front of Randy. That had definitely earned him a few points. But he was still on probation.

Not real probation, thank God—not like Randy, who couldn't leave the county without clearing it with his corrections officer. That was another point in Rod's favor.

"I could use a beer," she said.

Rod pointed toward the gleaming steel boiler at the lower end of the yard. "There's probably a keg down there," he said. "I'll be right back." Before she could tell him not to abandon her among these clam-eaters, he had plunged away through the crowd, slapping shoulders and shaking hands every step of the way like some shirt-sleeve politician.

A pair of middle-aged men closed in on her at once, drawing her forward from the driveway to the lawn, forward into the general swirl of conversation. Her high heels plugged quickly in the damp ground, rooting her in place.

"I'm Bill Rohrbaugh," said the pudgier of the two, balancing a plate of clamshells on his left forearm. "I'm with Continental Containers."

"Brenda Glass."

He pumped her arm enthusiastically, sending his plate clattering to the ground. Brenda frowned down at the mess. "Oh, don't worry about that," he said. "I was about finished anyway. And there's plenty more." He bent over to sop the freckles of lemon juice and melted butter from his loafers, and his broad scalp flushed red with the strain.

"I'm Dean Ballantine," said the other man.

Bill Rohrbaugh pulled himself upright and clapped a hand on Dean Ballantine's shoulder, partly from friendliness, it seemed, but mostly to hold himself steady. "Dean's his title, by the way, not his name."

"I'm with the medical school," Dean Ballantine explained.

"Is your husband in the tournament?" Bill Rohrbaugh asked.

"I'm here with Rod."

"Ah," they both said, nodding.

"Well," Bill Rohrbaugh said, "I'm here with my daughter. She's a sophomore up at State."

"Is she in the tournament?" Brenda asked. She briefly caught sight of Rod, but lost him again behind a drifting cluster of sinewy, suntanned old women.

Bill Rohrbaugh laughed. "Oh, hell no, she's no golfer. I just brought her along so we could check out some of the local colleges. She didn't like any of her classes this year, so she's thinking about maybe transferring to a smaller school." He took a gulp of his beer. "Got any recommendations?"

"I don't know," Brenda said. She shouldn't have let Rod bring her here. Her dress was too low-cut for this crowd; too many eyes were singling her out. She folded her arms over her breasts. "If she doesn't like school maybe she ought to drop out, get a job. Maybe wait tables or something."

Both men chuckled as if she'd said something witty, and then fell silent. Dean Ballantine continued to smile at her, while Bill Rohrbaugh began to nudge the blue-white clam-shells with his shoe.

"I'm ready for more clams," he said suddenly. "Anybody else want some?"

"I don't eat clams," Brenda said.

Bill Rohrbaugh eyed her suspiciously. "Why not? What's wrong with clams?"

Brenda slapped at a mosquito on her arm. "I don't know. It just seems unnatural to pry a thing out of its shell and eat it."

"But that's the fun part," he insisted. "It's like buying factory-direct. And let me tell you, these shells are great natural packaging." He shook his head in admiration. "Sometimes Mother Nature hits it right on the button."

"Not for me."

"Oh, yeah? What about these pearls?" he asked, pointing to the plastic strand around her neck. "I bet you'd pry open plenty of clams if you thought there were pearls inside."

"That's different," she told him.

"Actually," said Dean Ballantine, "you'd be wasting your time. Clams produce a very low-quality pearl. Almost worthless."

"Is that so," said Bill Rohrbaugh, rolling his eyes.

"Yes, it is, as a matter of fact. Their aragonite crystals are too large," he explained. "The pearls lack iridescence."

"Anyway," said Brenda, "I don't eat food that smells bad, and I think clams stink."

"Well, this batch sure does," Dean Ballantine agreed, craning his neck forward and lowering his voice. "I think they're a little overripe. Potato salad or coleslaw might be the safer way to go, Bill."

Bill twisted his face into an exaggerated scowl, and she began to sense how drunk he was. "Not for me, boy. I don't get to do this but once a year, so stink or no stink, I'm going back for seconds. Maybe even thirds." He took a plaid hand-kerchief from his back pocket and blew his nose. "Besides, my allergies have got me all blocked up. I can't smell a thing." He stepped carefully away from the scattered shells and set off toward the column of steam billowing from the clam pot across the yard.

Dean Ballantine moved a step closer. Even with his sun-baked skin, he wasn't a bad-looking guy. He was neat, trim, and well pressed—dapper, that was the word. The air around them was still muggy with leftover heat, but he looked twenty degrees cooler than anything she'd seen all day. He wore a peach-colored sweater draped over his shoulders, the empty sleeves tied loosely together across his chest, making it look as if he were being hugged lovingly from behind.

"I know what you mean about digging the clams out of their shells," he said. "I mean, it is their home, after all."

She pegged him quickly: another divorced asshole on the make. His smile was too kind, his eyes too filled with concern, as if each boiled clam were a lost patient who should have come to him sooner. Brenda gave him a noncommittal nod and slapped at the mosquito boring into the back of her hand.

He turned his profile to her and spoke toward the clam table. "It must come as quite a shock," he said. "Being boiled alive like that, I mean."

"Well, if clams can be surprised, I guess that'd do it."

"You know, it probably took the species millions of years to develop that shell for protection. Then we come along and just bypass the whole defense system—plop it in a pot hotter than any clam could imagine. It's a shame, really. All that evolution gone completely to waste."

"Sometimes I could use a shell myself," Brenda said, waving a pair of mosquitoes from her face.

Dean Ballantine bit his thumbnail thoughtfully. "Yeah, once that sun starts down, the insects really swarm. They've been especially bad all week. The rain had them breeding like flies."

"I suppose it would," Brenda said.

He sipped delicately at his beer. "Mosquitoes have the worst reputation," he said, snatching one from the air as he spoke and slapping it against his checkered trousers. "But I'll tell you the truth: it's fireflies that give me the creeps."

"How could fireflies bother anybody?"

He sighed and took another sip of beer. "That's one curse of knowledge, I guess. Just about anything in nature can turn your stomach if you get to know it well enough. That's why so few people go into the biological sciences." He leaned closer, crowding her with a too sweet smell of bottled spices. "In fact, it's probably the reason you're not a doctor right now yourself."

Brenda couldn't begin to count all the reasons she wasn't a doctor, but she knew squeamishness wasn't one of them.

"I think I pulled a D in biology," she told him. "But it wasn't because I got grossed out. I just couldn't remember the names of the worm parts."

Dean Ballantine pursed his lips as if he were thinking this over. "You're right," he said. "There's too much triviality to put up with."

Was that what she'd said?

He pointed to the low side of the yard, where already the first few fireflies were rising above the hedgerow. "You see that flashing? You know what that is?"

"Something to do with sex probably." A safe bet, since that was what guys always wanted to talk about. She didn't know if it was because sex was their only clear reference point, or if there was something about her in particular that kept urging the subject forward. In any case, she was sick of it.

Well, not entirely sick of it.

"Sex, that's right," Dean Ballantine said. "The female flashes at a certain frequency, and the appropriate male flies down to mate with her. But you know what happens after the male leaves?"

Sure, she knew.

"The female gets hungry," he went on, his milky eyes widening with awe. "So she changes her frequency. She sends out a false signal to attract some other male. When the new male flies down to her, she eats him."

He was right: if it was true, it was an unsettling thing to know. But at the same time she felt oddly encouraged, as if her team had scored a run.

Dean Ballantine took a gulp of his beer and dabbed the foam from his upper lip. "There's a lesson in that for all of us," he said.

She didn't know what lesson he meant, but she figured he was about to segue into the wife who'd neglected him or the kids who showed no respect or the job that was driving him to an early grave. She knew those songs by heart. In fact, she'd have welcomed a brief chorus or two: familiar lyrics were always a comfort. Besides, she'd found that one of the best times for her to think about her own problems was while some self-centered gasbag was droning on about his.

And she did have a problem to think about: Rod. He'd never been one of the tavern regulars, so she didn't know much about him. She'd only talked to him twice, and that second time he'd said he might want to marry her. What kind of a guy brought up marriage after just two conversations? He was either crazy or he was a jerk. Worse yet, he might be both, in which case she'd have to be especially careful: crazy jerks had always been her weakness. If he brought up marriage again, she might say yes just to see what would fall out of the tree.

Dean Ballantine said something else, but his words slipped into the blurry background of everyone else's conversations, and she missed his meaning. He looked at her expectantly, though, which annoyed her, and she might have said something ugly, purely out of reflex, if Rod hadn't suddenly reemerged from the crowd, an overfilled beer cup dripping from each hand.

"Hi, Doc," he said. "I see you've met Brenda."

The doc flicked a mosquito from his tanned forearm. "We were just discussing insects," he said.

"At least there was a breeze on the course today," Rod said. "That kept the mosquitoes off balance."

"The doc's afraid of fireflies," Brenda said, taking one of the beers.

Doc Ballantine laughed, but she could tell he was embarrassed. "Only in an abstract sense," he explained. "I reject the aesthetics of their lifestyle."

"I used to catch fireflies when I was a kid," Brenda said. "I'd wait until they flashed, and then pinch off their fire— you know, the jelly part, the part that glows. When you do that, the jelly stays lit. Then I'd stick it on the back of my finger like a big diamond ring."

"Sounds pretty weird," said Rod. "But I guess it's no worse than threading a cricket onto a fishhook."

Doc Ballantine managed a disinterested smile, then checked his wrist for the time. He wasn't wearing a watch, but the gesture itself seemed to give him the information he needed. "It's getting a little late for me," he said. "I think I'll head on home." He scanned the gathering for a moment, then turned back to Rod. "If our host ever shows up, thank him for me."

"Sure," said Rod. "Good luck in the tournament tomorrow."

"That's what it takes, all right. Luck'll beat skill any day. That's the one thing I hate about golf." He set his half-empty cup on a cluttered picnic table and headed down the driveway.

Brenda stared out across the crowd. "No host, huh? I guess that lets us out of Communion."

"What?"

"Nothing. Catholic joke. Never mind."

"Are you Catholic?"

She shouldn't have opened her mouth. "I don't know what I am." She steadied herself against Rod's arm and carefully unplugged her heels from the lawn. "I wore the wrong shoes," she said. "I need to sit down."

Rod led her up onto the patio to a pair of aluminum lawn chairs, and she settled herself cautiously onto one of the rickety frames. "So what's the story on this host?" she asked. "Why isn't he here?"

"His name's Lyle Davies," Rod told her. "Lyle's a local real estate agent. And I don't know where he is." He reached down with his paper napkin and wiped the chunks of mud from Brenda's heels as if her legs were golf clubs. "He's probably out looking for his wife. Shirley went a little nuts at the golf course this morning."

"What does that mean?"

"She tried to cement some of the holes shut. I had to send the grounds crew out to reset the cups."

"Why would she do a thing like that?"

"She didn't say. But I think she was mad because women weren't allowed in the tournament."

"Well, good for her, then."

"But now Glen Hanshaw wants the Board to revoke her Club membership. You probably haven't met Glen. He's Harold Hanshaw's father."

"Yeah, I know who he is," she said. "The Cadillac dealer. I told you, he sold me a bum used car when I was sixteen." She shook her head. "So can he just throw people out like that?"

"Well, Glen's the Club president, and most things seem to

get done his way. In fact, it was his idea to bar women from the tournament. But who knows? It might all blow over. Glen's mind has been kinda spotty lately. Tomorrow he might not remember a thing about it."

Brenda watched the mob of people milling around the yard. Everyone seemed so tidy and well groomed, like the people in television commercials, and the air was thick with manufactured smells—flowery, fruity minglings of after-shaves and colognes and beauty soaps and perfumes and skin lotions. Rod was right: there was nothing to be afraid of in this crowd. She couldn't have felt less threatened if she'd been in a wax museum.

"So this is what you do," she said.

"This is part of it," he answered. "For the time being, anyway. Sometimes I think it might be good to move on. Maybe try the PGA tour again." He started to say something more, but frowned suddenly at the lawn chair across from them.

Brenda frowned, too. A neatly severed bird's head was snared in the plastic webbing. A pigeon's head, it looked like, cloaked in a cloud of mosquitoes and flies.

A sign of the times, her mother would have called it.

The golf course was a beautiful place at night, she had to grant him that. Once her eyes had adjusted to the dark-ness, she could see every sculpted detail, every trimmed bush and shining sand trap. She could even make out flag-sticks flopping in the breeze two hundred yards away. Every-thing stood crystal-clear—though nothing had a color. Shades and shadows, that was all. Like an X ray of the world.

Rod had encouraged her to take off her shoes to walk the greens and fairways, and she was amazed at the silkiness of the ground. There were no stones, or sticks, or briars; no saw grass, or sharp roots, or tin-can lids; nothing but cool dewfall in the soft shoots of grass.

She'd half expected to end up here. It was a standard ploy of every guy she'd ever dated. They all wanted to show her the places they worked. Familiar territory gave them enough confidence to make their move, she understood that. Over the years she'd had private tours of the shoe factory, the self-storage warehouse, the security office at the Holiday Inn, a couple of fast-food kitchens, a Mayflower moving van, and a Fotomat booth. Randy took her to the garage on their first date and ruined her good blouse on the grease rack. The golf course was the best so far, but she wasn't about to get any grass stains on her gown—especially since Rod had been dumb enough to bring her here straight from the clambake instead of getting her some real dinner first.

"I guess you probably live in one of those places," she said, pointing to the sprawling homes that lined the distant border of the course. Even in the darkness, they had ele-gance and charm.

"Those mostly belong to the Club members," he told her. "I couldn't afford to live like that in a hundred years."

"I thought golf pros were loaded."

She could see him smile in the shadows. "Only the good ones. The ones like me live in apartment complexes out by the Interstate. And we tend to fall behind in our rent."

She felt the gap between them narrow.

"My job's only got one fringe benefit," he went on. "I get to pretend that I own the golf course."

"Pretending's important," she said. "When I sing with the band, I like to pretend that I own the stage."

"I've heard you sing," he told her. "As far as I'm concerned, you do own the stage."

"Thanks," she said, though she felt disappointed. She didn't want Rod to be a fan. Fans were fickle and stupid, taken in by every cheap bauble and dyed feather. With fans, there would always be the day of disillusionment. Idols would ultimately be cast out—she still remembered that much from the Song of Solomon, which her mother had once made her read ten times as a punishment for cutting her hair. Her mother had always punished her with Bible verses, sometimes forcing her to reread the same dry passages for hours until she'd known them by heart. The Song of Solomon had turned out to be her favorite. Her mother had believed it was about Christ's love for the church, but that wasn't what Brenda saw there. For her, it was about men loving women.

The whine of a siren rose in the distance, almost beyond hearing. It tingled through the hair on the back of her neck. "Sounds like someone's got problems," she said.

"What do you mean?"

"The siren."

He paused a few seconds. "Yeah, I hear it now. Speeders on the highway, I guess."

"Ambulance," she corrected him. Did he really know so little about sirens? She'd thought everyone could tell an ambulance from a cop car, and the state cops from city and county. Rod must have lived a cushy life to have never learned that language.

They came to a bench beneath a broad, dark tree and sat down together facing the winding lane of houses. Each house was different, and each had a yard as big as the block she lived on.

"This is the high point," Rod said. "You can see just about the whole course from up here."

Brenda felt the cool aluminum slats of the bench through her gown. The siren was growing louder.

"Is your boyfriend still in the hospital?" Rod asked.

She'd known the question was coming—or at least something like it. Men always wanted to know how far the last guy was out the door.

"I don't know," she told him. "Anyway, he's not my boyfriend anymore."

She hated to give Rod such a straight answer, but she

didn't feel like playing games this time. Randy was too dangerous for that.

"He really took a beating," Rod said.

Brenda sighed. "He usually does. Randy's got weak bones, so he can't take a punch. But last night was about the worst I've seen. That biker just took him apart."

"What do you mean, weak bones?"

"I mean he does a lot of speed. Speed sucks the calcium out of your system. That's why his teeth are so bad." She thought of Randy lying on his side in the tavern parking lot, a few bloody teeth scattered around him on the asphalt like chunks of gravel. The memory warmed her. She'd waited months for that moment—the moment of finding him so badly damaged that she could tell him they were through without worrying what he might do to her. *Better is the end of a thing than the beginning thereof.* Where was that from? Somewhere in Ecclesiastes, she remembered; but chapter and verse were lost to her now. She just couldn't call up the numbers like she used to, not without her mother around to spot-check her all the time. Anyway, Rod had come along at an opportune time, and she'd boarded him like a train in a burning station. "He lost some big ones last night," she went on. "Molars. I took a couple of them along to the hospital in case the doctors could stick 'em back in, but they were all too rotten to mess with. That fight probably saved him a few toothaches down the road."

"Does he know he's not your boyfriend anymore?"

"Yeah. I told him in the emergency room while he was filling out forms."

"I guess he was pretty upset."

"I think he was. But he had a lot of gauze in his mouth, so I couldn't make out too much of what he said." She felt suddenly exposed. "You probably think I'm terrible, dumping him at a time like that."

"No. I just wonder how you ever got mixed up with him in the first place."

"I got really stoned at a party one night," she said. "Randy was there, and I figured, what the hell, it might work out. He looked all right." She knew this portion of the truth didn't cast her in a very good light, but every audience was different and had to be sounded out. Honesty could be a smart tactic if she used it early enough. It might keep the act from dying later on.

"Anyway, I'm glad you got out of it," Rod said. "I'm glad it's over."

"Yeah, well, the payments don't stop when you wreck your car," she said. She put her shoes on the bench between them and rubbed her eyes. She didn't like thinking about Randy.

The ambulance rounded the corner at the far end of the lane and moved slowly along the row of houses, sweeping a bright red arc across the golf-course grounds.

"That driver looks lost," Rod said.

"He's checking house numbers," Brenda told him as the

ambulance pulled into the driveway of a large two-story co-
lonial. The siren died away, but was replaced immediately by
a harsh animal sound, something like the braying of a don-
key. The attendants climbed down from the ambulance and
walked quickly around to the front of the house.

"What's making that awful noise?" Brenda asked.

"A mule," Rod told her. "That's Glen Hanshaw's place.
He keeps a bunch of old mules in his back yard. The siren
must have spooked one."

Brenda strained her eyes to see the mules, but couldn't
make out much in the yard—just dark, lumpy shadows beneath the trees. "Why does he keep mules?"

Rod shook his head and laced his fingers between hers.
"Beats me. The truth is, I don't think I've figured out why
anybody does anything." He moved her shoes aside and slid
closer to her on the bench.

Brenda knew why people did things. Food and sex covered most of it. People would do anything to feed those basic
hungers. Beyond that, there was guilt. Fistfights, mules,
failed relationships—hunger and guilt framed every picture,
shaped all the odd leaps in people's lives, she was sure of it.
The hungers you could satisfy, sometimes, if you were lucky,
but guilt was trickier to live with. You could hide from it,
argue with it, lie to it, pretend to laugh at it, or just suffer
under it, but you couldn't get away from it, not on your best
day. Some of it you could atone for, she imagined—she
believed—but only for little pieces of it. Never all of it.

Nobody could get rid of all of it; there were always chunks left over, no matter what you did. Her mother had taught her that, and so had the nuns for all ten years of her schooling. There were saints and martyrs; and then there were the guilty.

Even her singing convicted her—though that had once been her one undeniable gift, the gift not even her mother had been able to ignore. *Sing unto the Lord a new song,* her mother had urged her, reveling in the Psalmist's rapture. But the Lord had never come around with any contracts, so Brenda learned to sing the old stuff instead, blues and torch mostly; and she sang it anyplace she could pick up a few bucks, no matter what the clientele. She'd liked it that way at first—the freedom of singing only for herself had been exhilarating. But now she wasn't so sure. These days it seemed she wasn't singing for herself at all: she was singing for the roughnecks and dropouts who crowded into smoky rooms, fixing her in their half-lidded stares. She was singing for the men who wanted her song. *And they that wasted us required of us mirth, saying, Sing . . .*

She would probably turn out to be guilty with Rod, just as she knew she'd been guilty with Randy—and the ones before Randy. For as long as she could remember, every new man in her life had turned out to be a punishment for the men she'd known before. But she kept looking. She had to keep looking. There was always that chance of sudden grace.

A burst of light erupted from the back of the house, followed by a sharp, echoing pop. The braying mule fell silent.

"Well, that was odd," Rod said.

Brenda shifted on the bench. "I think somebody just shot that mule in the head."

"That doesn't seem likely," he said, though he offered no better explanation.

"Maybe Shirley Davies is crazier than you thought," she suggested.

There was another flash, another loud pop. The two attendants scrambled back inside their ambulance and squealed down the driveway. They drove about a hundred yards along the lane and stopped.

"I hate like hell to say this," Rod said, getting up from the bench, "but I think I'd better go look in on Glen and Harold and see what the trouble is. Will you be all right here for a little while?"

"I'm all right anywhere." She stood up and hooked her arm through his. "But let's check with the ambulance guys before you go ringing any doorbells."

They angled across the fairway toward the pulsing red light, then cut through the back yard of a home three lots down from Glen Hanshaw. Brenda noticed a pair of silhouettes behind the curtains of an upstairs bedroom window. Rod saw them, too, and waved his arm in reassurance.

"It's okay, Clarence!" he called.

A man leaned his bald head out the window. "Is that you, Rod?"

"Yeah. With a friend."

"What the hell's going on?"

"I don't know yet. Some kind of trouble down at Glen's place. Somebody called an ambulance."

"There's been a lot of racket over there tonight," Clarence said. "You tell the old bastard we're tired of those goddamn mules."

"All right, Clarence, I'll tell him."

"No, you won't," said Clarence. "Nobody will. That's the whole goddamn problem. And stay the hell out of my flower beds. I just had the landscapers in." He ducked his head back inside, and Rod and Brenda picked their way carefully up through Clarence's side yard to the street, where the men in the ambulance were quietly watching the Hanshaw place in their rearview mirrors.

"Evening," Rod said. The man on the passenger side jumped.

"Jesus, don't sneak up on me like that," he said. He took a couple of breaths and frowned out at them. "What do you want?"

"We just wondered what's going on," Rod said.

"Christ, Del," he said to the driver, "can't we go anywheres without gawkers coming out of the woodwork?"

"We're not gawkers," Rod said. "We're friends of the Hanshaws, and we just want to know if anything's wrong."

"Well, Jesus, buddy, take your best guess. This here's an ambulance, for christ's sake."

Del punched his partner in the arm and leaned across him to the passenger window. "You gotta excuse Joe. We been on a long shift, and he's had a lot of caffeine." Joe rubbed his arm and scowled down at the floorboard. "We got a call that somebody got cut on some glass," Del explained.

"So how come you're just sitting here?" Rod asked.

"Gunshots, man," Joe told him. "We don't go in when there's guns involved."

"There might have been some gunshots," Del conceded.

"So you just sit here?" Brenda asked.

"No, ma'am," said Del. "What we do is we radio in for police assistance. They go in first to scope out the situation —that's policy. Then it's our turn." He nodded out toward the darkness. "They oughta be along anytime now."

"I don't hear any sirens," Brenda said.

They all paused to listen. There was no noise but the soft, idling rumble of the ambulance itself. Even the crickets were quiet.

"This is stupid," Rod said. "I'll check it out myself." He squeezed Brenda lightly on the arm and started toward the Hanshaw house.

"Suit yourself," said Joe. "But if you get shot, don't come crying to us about it."

Brenda had left her shoes on the bench and couldn't walk the gravel-strewn road as easily as the golf course, so she fell behind as Rod moved briskly down the lane. She called to him as he reached the edge of the Hanshaw driveway, and he paused beneath the purpled light of the streetlamp. When she caught up with him, he smiled apologetically.

"Maybe you'd better stay here," he said. "If Glen's in a bad state of mind, we don't want to spring any strangers on him."

Rod went to the door and rang the bell once, politely, as if he were a dinner-party guest. Finally, the front door opened and a stooped old man squinted out at Rod through the storm-door screen. They talked briefly—too low for Brenda to make out what was said—then the old man pushed the storm door open and ushered Rod into the house.

She stood there for a couple of long minutes, listening. Now that she was away from the ambulance she could hear other noises—locusts in the trees, air conditioners, even the wind combing the roadside grass. But there were still no police sirens from the highway, and no more gunshots from the house or yard.

Suddenly a figure darted around the rear corner of the house and raced across the dark side yard. Brenda's first impulse was to run herself, but since she had nowhere to go, she held her ground. When it dawned on her that the runner was Rod, she panicked even more. But then she realized he wasn't running *from* the house, he was running *toward* the ambulance, probably taking Joe and Del the explanation that would allow them to go in and help. She looked again at the quiet house: nothing had changed.

After a few words with Rod, Del shifted the ambulance noisily into reverse and accelerated toward her, weaving awkwardly between the grassy shoulders of the lane. At the entrance to the Hanshaw driveway he swung too wide and clipped the mailbox, then crushed a juniper bush as he backed up to the porch. Both Del and Joe hopped out and circled to the rear of the ambulance, where they retrieved their various kits and pieces of equipment, then disappeared into the house. By then Rod had jogged up beside her. He was carrying a rifle.

"What's going on?" she asked.

"Nothing criminal," he said. "But it's pretty ugly."

"What happened?"

"A freak accident. Glen and Harold were out back on the glassed-in patio, and apparently some of the mules started to act up. One of them kicked through the plate-glass wall right where Harold was standing. It cut him up pretty bad."

"So what's the gun for?"

"Show-and-tell," he said. "I figured the ambulance guys needed some kind of proof that everything was under control. So I made Glen give me this." He held the rifle up between them. It gleamed under the streetlamp, and Brenda could smell the oddly clean mixture of oil and spent gunpowder. "It's a twenty-two Hornet," Rod said. "I used one like it once when I was a kid. It'll pop a groundhog at three hundred yards."

"But what were the shots about?"

Rod pointed toward the back yard, though there was nothing to see but the darkness. "When Harold got hurt, I guess Glen sorta freaked out. He put down all six of his mules."

"But there were only two shots," she said.

"After the first five mules, he ran out of bullets and had to go look for his cartridge box. All we caught was the end of the show." Rod shook his head and sighed. "It won't be easy to get rid of those carcasses either, I can tell you that. Come Monday, things'll smell pretty stiff around here."

The police siren began its whine a mile or more away.

"I'd better take this back inside," Rod said, looking down at the gun.

"Are you sure that's a good idea?" Brenda asked.

"Well, I can't just walk off with it. And anyway, I want to check on Harold." He seemed embarrassed, as if he thought the whole mess was somehow his fault. Was that how it always had to be? Were we still guilty even when we acted right?

Rod carried the rifle around the front of the ambulance toward the front door. The siren grew louder for a moment, then began to fade, and Brenda realized that the cop car—a county car, it was, from the Sheriff's Department—had missed the turn and was now cruising a parallel road a quarter of a mile away. At the same time it occurred to her that when the deputies did finally show up, Rod had better not be walking around with Glen Hanshaw's rifle.

Randy would have known a thing like that instinctively, but Rod was a different species; he'd stand there looking sheepish and get his head blown off, not understanding, as any police officer would, that sometimes it's a shoot-first world, with guilt and innocence overlapping.

For that matter, some hair-triggered deputy—or maybe even the sheriff himself—could probably shoot any one of them and not be far wrong. *For the heart is deceitful above all things, and desperately wicked. Who shall know it?* That had been one of her mother's favorites—and no wonder. Jeremiah was the most downbeat of the prophets. He saw no hope at all.

As she hurried across the lawn to warn Rod about the snap judgments of deputies, Joe and Del came out onto the porch and removed a gurney from the back of the ambulance. She held the storm door for them, then followed them into the house.

The place looked neater, much less chaotic than she had expected. Tapestried pillows lined the back of the brocade couch, and porcelain bird statues rested undisturbed on the piano. The portraits of two boys—one of them Harold, she guessed, painted some forty years ago—hung straight above the mantel, illuminated by a pair of small brass lamps. The only sign that anything was wrong was the trail of dark spots that cut diagonally across the white carpet, stretching from the kitchen doorway to the telephone table in the entry hall, where she now stood. The spots pooled here into a single broad stain. By the look of it, Harold had called for the ambulance himself.

She moved through the living room and kitchen to the back of the house, where all five men were gathered on the now exposed patio. The floor was littered with sparkling shards of glass, and the hairy brown back of a mule bulged across the bottom frame of the rear wall. Harold lay on the gurney, pale and bloated as a plaster Buddha, already half mummied in bandages. The tourniquet on his thigh was clearly makeshift—a flowered pillowcase tightened with a barbecue fork—but his stomach, chest, and shoulder were a patchwork of gauze and adhesive tape. Joe and Del passed a pair of straps over his chest and knees and buckled him in place. She was surprised at how quickly they'd dressed Harold's wounds—a couple of professionals, after all. Glen Hanshaw sat talking to himself in a lounge chair. Rod stood before the dead mule, cradling the gun in his arms like some mountain man protecting his kill. She'd been right to come inside.

"Hey, Harold," she said, pausing in the kitchen doorway. "How's it going?"

Harold turned his head slightly and stared hard at her, unable at first to place her face. "Brenda," he said finally. "Brenda, from the tavern."

"You got it."

He looked puzzled. "Did my father call you?"

"No, sport, we were just in the neighborhood. How do you feel?"

"A little drained," he said, slipping into a feeble laugh.

"I tried to call," Glen said suddenly. "But the hospital wasn't there. Some woman came on and told me it was nine-oh-five P.M. She said it was eighty-four degrees."

Harold shook his head. "It's okay, Dad. Everything's fine."

Glen kicked at the glass around his feet, sending a few jagged fragments tinkling across the tile floor. "We won't clean this up tonight," he said. "We'll start fresh in the morning."

Joe and Del lifted the gurney up into the kitchen. "Mr. Hanshaw, why don't you come along with us," Del suggested.

"Sure thing," he said brightly. "What kind of car do you boys drive?" Rod helped the old man to his feet and led him through the broken glass. The sheriff's siren was much closer now, maybe a block or two away.

"Here, let me help you with this," Brenda said, carefully taking the Hornet from Rod's hand. It was of a lighter weight than the shotguns Randy kept around his place. She clicked on the safety, then checked the chamber for shells.

Glen nodded his approval. "That's right, never leave a loaded gun in the house." He looked at the dead mule bordering his patio. "I had to shoot that Missouri twice, you know. But he was a mean one anyway. Bad teeth."

"Take it easy, Harold," Rod said as Del maneuvered the gurney into the living room. "I'll look in on you tomorrow."

"Tomorrow's the last day of the tournament," Glen said. "We'd all better get a good night's sleep."

Joe took Glen by the elbow. "Let's go now, Mr. Hanshaw. Let's go get everybody checked out."

"Checked in, you mean," he said, stepping up into the kitchen. "You know, it was a sad thing for me to shoot those mules. But if an animal turns on you, it's got to be destroyed. My daddy taught me that."

As Glen and Joe followed the gurney to the front of the house, the sheriff's car pulled up outside. Brenda laid the Hornet on the tile countertop and took Rod by the arm.

"Interesting date," she said. "Where do we go from here? The sheriff's office or the slaughterhouse?"

"Let's go back to the golf course," Rod said. "I don't want to get tied up with the police about this."

"Fine with me. I need to get my shoes anyway."

He helped her over the dead Missouri and led her slowly

down through the back yard. Their eyes were new to the darkness now, so they kept to the patches of spilled patio light to avoid the other carcasses. By the time they'd climbed the fence at the low end of the Hanshaw yard, the ambulance was speeding away down the lane, its siren rising again into an urgent howl. The police—the deputies or whoever —moved noisily around inside the house, banging doors, talking, and crunching through broken glass. Brenda felt relieved they'd slipped away.

As she walked with Rod up the long hill to retrieve her shoes, the fairway grass again turned soft beneath her feet and gradually her eyes readjusted to the night. When they reached the bench, she turned back toward the house, seeing it more clearly than she had before. The charm was gone; the dark lumps spotting the lawn seemed more obscene now than mysterious. Maybe Dean Ballantine was right: maybe it was a bad idea to look at anything too closely.

"Let's go get some dinner," Rod said, handing Brenda her shoes. "It's still early."

She felt tired to the bone. Rod was a sweet guy, but it wasn't early, not at all. Early had left her long ago; she'd squandered it over a long history of blind leaps on stony ground. Now she was almost played out. The last two thousand years had deadened her reflexes; she couldn't catch a moment like she used to.

The late Brenda Glass, that's what it was all coming down to, that's what she was starting to become. She might have no more future than a clam dropped in a pot, or an old mule trapped in a crazy man's yard.

Still, there was that outside chance: grace might come when a person least deserved it. "Dinner can wait," she said, tossing her shoes onto the grass. She stood in front of him, her back to the moonlight, and slipped the sequined straps from her shoulders. Then she slid the dress down over her hips and let it pile softly at her feet. Rod didn't say anything, didn't move, or even breathe—but that was all right. She knew him well enough by now. More than that, she knew the power her nakedness had. Flesh was a straightforward thing, the only answer she had ever learned to live with. *All flesh is grass,* her mother had warned her, *and the goodliness thereof is as the flower of the field.*

But what kind of warning was that? Did it mean that there wasn't much good in the flesh, that it offered too few flowers per acre? Or did it mean the flower was what mattered most and should be cultivated?

In any case, she'd made her choice: flesh was the ticket she could best afford. It might not take her as far as she'd like; and someday it was bound to fail her altogether, time being time and dust being dust. But for now it worked, and that was no small thing. For now, it could still seal a bargain.

Music for Hard Times

Jimmy swept the last bits of loose turf into his dustpan and slowly scanned the pro-shop floor: it still looked filthy. Two hundred golfers had tracked the mud in all day long, and now their grimy traffic-ways branched from the doorway like shadows, darkening each aisle. Sweeping couldn't clean that kind of dirt; he'd have to wash the whole floor with a scrub brush and ammonia.

He didn't mind, though. The extra work gave him an excuse to stay late, and staying late gave him the opportunity to go through the members' golf bags for loose change. On a good Sunday night he could fish out thirty or forty bucks, no sweat, which gave him just the boost he needed to cover his food bills and his rent. It was a

great fringe benefit to a job he already thought was perfect.

Absolutely perfect. Why else would he have passed up college to stay here? When Dickinson offered him the golf scholarship, he had almost taken it. But then he realized that a chance to play college golf wasn't reason enough to leave. He could play all the golf he wanted right here. Rod had made him the assistant pro, and that meant free greens fees for as long as he kept his job. He took advantage of it, too, spending more time on the course than the richest members of the Club. Scrubbing an occasional late-night floor was a small price to pay for all that.

And so what if it had pissed his father off?

He found the steel bucket under the sink in the mop closet and had just filled it with hot water when he heard a sharp tapping on one of the windows out front. "We're closed," he shouted, and poured some cleaner into the bucket. The tapping came again, louder this time and more insistent, but he ignored it. He'd worked here long enough to know what to expect on the last night of a tournament: drunks on the prowl. One or two always managed to drift down from the closing dinner-dance when the polka band broke after its first set. They'd think because the pro-shop light was on they could come in and browse, maybe pick up a cheap new sweater for the wife. But Rod never left him the key to the cash drawer, so there wasn't much he could do but shoo people away. Sometimes, though, they were hard to get rid of, especially once he'd let them in the shop. He tried his best not to despise them.

The older guys were harmless enough—they just got talkative when they got tanked up and always battered him with lame advice: he should stick with school and get a good education, he should make the most of his youth, he should get regular dental checkups. Sometimes they'd crack some feeble joke, or quiz him on the generic details of his life. It all followed a pretty standard drill—that avuncular Middle-American posturing he'd expect from any grade school principal, Bible salesman, or TV weatherman.

The younger drunks were a different story. The guys in their late twenties or early thirties seemed to want to prove they were still nineteen, like Jimmy, and if he let them get a foot in the door, it was all he could do to keep them from trashing the place. Most of them acted pissed off about their lives—their jobs weren't making them rich, their golf scores weren't low enough, their drug connections weren't reliable, and their wives were starting to catch on to what shits they were. The young drunks were the ones who worried him, because he knew where they were headed.

He dropped a scrub brush into the ammonia water and lifted the bucket from the sink, sloshing a warm wave over the rim onto his sneakers. He stood for a moment in the doorway listening: muted fragments of an accordion tune strayed unevenly through the bank of closed windows, the faint notes mingling with highway noise and distant bursts of clubhouse laughter. The tapping had stopped, but now he could hear voices rising in conversation on the pro-shop porch, and Jimmy knew he was stuck. Single drunks tended to wander away if he ignored them, but when they came in pairs they were more tenacious, clinging doggedly to their own fuzzy game plans regardless of what he said or did.

He carried the bucket to the front of the shop and set it on the rubber mat by the door. As he reached into the gray water for the scrub brush, one of the people on the porch began to rattle the storm door.

"Jimmy! Open up!"

He recognized Teddy Mumford's voice. Teddy was one of the high-profile members, partly because he was the Club's insurance agent and, at twenty-eight, had already back-slapped his way onto the Board of Directors. But he was also the current Club Champion, which gave him a certain standing. Jimmy had no problem with that—he'd played a couple of rounds with Teddy and knew what a great shotmaker he was. But there were other dimensions of Teddy's personality that Jimmy didn't care for.

For one thing, he happened to know that Teddy carried a nine-shot twenty-two pistol in his golf bag.

For another, Jimmy understood why.

Teddy was actually more a gambler than a golfer. He had a reputation for sandbagging—turning in high scores to run his handicap up—then conning his foursome into a high-stakes game. His standard bet was fifty dollars a hole, double on birdies, plus carryovers on all ties. Guys could drop a thousand bucks in games like that and never know what hit them. That left more than a few people unhappy, which was bad for the general atmosphere of the Club. But what made it worse was that Teddy also had a tendency to cheat. Nobody ever mentioned it, though, not to his face, because he also had a tendency to explode. Most of the locals had simply stopped playing with him. Still, around the clubhouse Teddy Mumford was a bulldozer of friendliness, and the people who didn't know him invariably liked him a lot.

Jimmy set the bucket aside and pulled open the front door. It was Mumford, all right, dressed in a white double-breasted suit and grinning like a long-lost relative. Moths flitted around his shoulders as if he were a source of light. A man and a woman stood behind him on the porch, but it was too dark for Jimmy to make out their faces. The man, he could tell, was pretty big.

"Jimmy-Boy! I knew you'd still be around." Teddy sounded even more jovial than usual.

"I'm washing the floor," Jimmy said, hoping that might relieve him of the obligation to invite anyone inside.

"Take a break," Teddy told him. "I want you to meet a couple of friends of mine." He reached out and rattled the aluminum door again. Jimmy had no choice but to unlock it.

Teddy stepped quickly inside and put his arm around Jimmy's shoulder. "A rock and a hard place," he said under his breath, and Jimmy had a vague sense that Mumford was apologizing for something that hadn't happened yet. "Jimmy Wickerham," he said, turning his smile to the couple now coming through the doorway, "This is Bill Rohrbaugh and his daughter, Willa. Bill was my partner in the tournament this weekend."

"Right, I remember," Jimmy said. "You bought a T-Line putter from me this morning."

A warm smile spread across Bill Rohrbaugh's weathered face. "Best investment I've made in years."

Jimmy wiped his wet palm on the side of his jeans and shook the man's outstretched hand. "Glad to meet you," he said, and then nodded politely to Willa. She seemed to be about his age, maybe a year older, and she smiled at him with a look of honest relief. Jimmy could understand that well enough: she'd probably spent the last two hours chewing dried-out chicken wings and watching a platoon of double-knit geezers do the polka.

"Jimmy's a great kid," Teddy announced, and playfully roughed his hair as if he were a favorite dog. Jimmy felt his face go red—he was too old to put up with that kind of condescending locker-room horseshit—but he knew better than to say anything. Willa was a good-looking girl, and he didn't want to rock the boat until he found out what the situation was.

"I hope you've had a good weekend," he said.

Mr. Rohrbaugh pulled a handkerchief from his pants pocket and blew his nose. "The golf was great," he said.

Then he turned to Teddy and started to say something else, but Willa cut him off.

"The rest of it's been pretty dismal," she said, crossing her arms over her breasts. Jimmy nodded and smiled. Her dress was the bare-shoulder kind he thought was pretty hot, and it was cut low enough to show the tan lines from her swimsuit. Her long hair had a silky look, and though the color might have seemed a dreary dishwater blond on someone else, on her it seemed radiant, not the least bit drab, each strand holding the light in a summertime chlorine glow. Her skin and teeth were flawless, which meant either good genes or good money—though genes were the long shot, given Bill Rohrbaugh's sagging bulk and the liver spots strung across his balding scalp. In fact, the only thing that kept Willa from seeming incredibly beautiful was that her father was standing next to her, demonstrating how ugly certain of her features might someday turn out to be. But that was natural: fathers could put anyone in a bad light, he knew that well enough. True, her nose might eventually broaden into her old man's terrier look, and when she hit middle age, she might be in line for about sixty of his extra pounds. But that didn't matter. On this balmy, clear night she looked like a prom queen's prom queen, even under the fluorescent lights, and it crossed Jimmy's mind, as it always did when he met a new girl or played a new course, that the world was full of exotic possibilities.

"Do you folks live around here?" He'd intended the

question as an icebreaker for Willa, but it was her father who stepped in with the answer.

"We're from up at Lock Haven," he said. "I'm the Human Resources Director at Continental Containers." He scanned the room for a moment, then pointed to the stack of new golf shoes beneath the windows. "That's one of our products right there."

"What? The Foot Joys?"

Mr. Rohrbaugh frowned. "No, not the shoes, the boxes. We make the packaging other companies put their products in. Everything from furniture crates to milk cartons. You name it, we've got a box for it."

"Listen," Teddy said, resting a hand on Mr. Rohrbaugh's round shoulder, "I've got to get a couple of things from my golf bag. Why don't you two browse around. If you see anything you like, Jimmy'll put it on my tab."

Mr. Rohrbaugh frowned. "I told you, I've got no interest in merchandise."

"I could use a sweater," Willa said, rubbing her hands up the backs of her arms. "It's chillier than I thought it would be."

"We're in a hollow," Jimmy explained. "There's a creek along the low side of the parking lot, and that cools the air down quicker. It's usually about five degrees colder here at night than it is in town."

Willa looked at him and smiled, but it was the smile of a tourist taking in the local color, and he felt his heart tighten.

"Fine, then," Mr. Rohrbaugh said. "My daughter'll take a sweater, and we'll knock off thirty bucks."

"They're thirty-eight dollars," Jimmy said, pointing to the shelf of women's sweaters along the rear wall. "But the register's already closed out."

"I said he could put it on my tab." Teddy's smile was so strained he looked demented. "You can write it up tomorrow."

Jimmy shrugged. "If you say so."

"Good man," said Teddy, clapping his hands together. He glanced briefly around the room as if he were trying to remember what to do next, and suddenly Jimmy was able to read just how drunk Teddy was. Not sloppy, but exuberant —slightly out of control. Jimmy had seen him this way before, and knew it was best not to cross him. After a couple of vodka tonics, Teddy tended to take an even narrower view of the world than usual, sizing up the people around him as either best friends or mortal enemies, with not much ground in between.

"That's right, your golf was great," Teddy said. He leveled a look at Jimmy. "We won the goddamn tournament— did you know that? The whole shebang. They gave us each a new set of woods and two dozen golf balls."

"Yeah, I heard about it. Congratulations."

"Old Bill here couldn't miss a putt all day with that new T-Line you sold him. Best he's ever played in his life. Isn't that right, Bill?"

"I had the touch all right."

Teddy leaned in close and tapped Jimmy on the chest with his forefinger. "The last hole: Bill knocks in a thirty-footer, and bingo! we beat out old man Guise and that bald-ass partner of his by one stroke. Guise was so mad he didn't know whether to shit or go blind." He paused to let this information sink in, and the four of them stood there in awkward silence. It was the first time Jimmy had ever seen Teddy Mumford run a conversation into a concrete wall. Teddy seemed to notice it, too, and stared self-consciously at the floor between them. Then, regaining his bearings, he snapped his head up suddenly and smiled. "Be right back," he said, and disappeared into the bag room.

"Well," said Jimmy, trying to pick up the slack, "I guess you guys made out okay."

Mr. Rohrbaugh blew his nose again, then folded the handkerchief neatly into quarters and tucked it into the breast pocket of his jacket. "Can't complain," he said.

Willa shook her head. "Well, I sure can." She turned abruptly and started toward the stack of women's sweaters.

"Willa's a little miffed," Mr. Rohrbaugh told him. "We were gonna check out some of the local colleges while we were here—that's why she came down with me. She hasn't been too happy up at State. But the tournament took more time than I thought, so we never got around to it."

"We could have skipped that stupid clambake," Willa said over her shoulder.

"She's right about that," he conceded. "We both had stomach pains all night long. I almost didn't play today."

"Are these all you've got?" she asked, holding up one of the lavender pullovers. "I'd rather have one with buttons."

"Sorry," Jimmy said. "That's all we've got."

Teddy leaned his head through the bag-room doorway. "Jimmy, could you give me a hand here? I can't find my golf bag."

"It's in your cubbyhole," Jimmy told him. "Top row, fourth from the right."

Teddy stared at him coldly. "Maybe you could show me."

Jimmy excused himself and followed Teddy back into the bag room, which was remarkably uncluttered considering the chaos of the past three days. There were still a few guests' golf bags crowded against the worktable, but all the members' clubs and bags had already been cleaned and put away. Jimmy had done most of the work himself, so he wasn't surprised to see that Teddy's bag was exactly where it was supposed to be. "There you go," he said, pointing to the cubbyhole.

Teddy didn't even glance at his bag. He carefully closed the door and listened for a moment at the jamb, then turned to Jimmy and beamed his standard ingratiating smile. "You're invited to a party," he said.

There was something odd in Mumford's tone, some twist of attitude Jimmy couldn't quite identify, and it left him feeling disoriented, as if he'd used the wrong iron for a routine shot. He had no desire to get tangled up in this volatile drunk's rat-brained plans; but he also had no desire to lose his job. He was already on thin ice with the Board of Directors because Mrs. Davies had accused him of losing some of her golf clubs. That made it a bad idea to disappoint a Board member right now, especially a vindictive jerk like Teddy Mumford.

And there was also Willa to consider. She smelled like air-conditioned flowers, perfect for the summer night, and he wouldn't mind a chance to make some kind of impression, even with her father hanging around. "When?" he asked.

"Now. Tonight."

"I've still got to wash the floor."

"That can wait." Teddy stepped in close to him. "Look, I'm not talking about some Country Club polka-fest. This guy I know is having a going-away bash up at his cabin on South Mountain. And he's hired a real band."

"Who?"

Mumford reached up and tightened the knot of his tie. "You don't know him."

"No, I mean who's the band?"

"The Radio Actives. I hear they're the best in the area."

Jimmy laughed. He'd heard the Radio Actives a couple of times around town. The guy on lead guitar had a few good riffs, but the drummer and the bass player were both lousy and the guy on keyboards couldn't keep his equipment from shorting out. "They're totally lame," he said. "Except for a couple of old Beatles songs, all they do is country-western."

Teddy took out his wallet and held it open. "You see this?" he asked, shaking it upside down to demonstrate its emptiness. "This is a major business problem."

Jimmy looked at the wallet. It was one of the most ornate he'd ever seen—new hand-tooled leather with a scene of stampeding horses embossed across the back and bits of polished turquoise mounted into the corners, each stone held in place by delicate silver brackets. The whole wallet bulged with business and credit cards and, even without cash, looked healthier than Jimmy's own billfold, which at the moment contained five dollars, a driver's license, and a YMCA pass. "I hope you're not asking me for a loan," he said.

Teddy waved his hand between them as if he were clearing away smoke. "Christ, no, that's not what I meant. I just want you to drive us to the party."

"Why me? Why don't you drive yourself?"

Teddy looked annoyed. "Because I'm drunk, for one thing. Any moron can see that." He took a deep breath and closed his eyes. "Anyway, you're a good kid and I'd like to have you along. You can keep what's-her-name entertained while I talk business with Bill. That shouldn't be such a chore." He opened his eyes and sagged back against a line of golf bags. Some loose clubs at the end of the row clanked against the sink and rattled to the floor, but Teddy didn't seem to notice. "Besides, you've got one of those Jeep four-wheel-drive things, don't you?"

"I've got an old Bronco."

"Perfect. This guy's cabin is out in the boonies, and his driveway's a little on the rough side. With all the rain we had last week, I don't think my Cadillac could handle the ruts."

"So skip it. Take them somewhere else. What's the big deal about a party in the woods?"

Teddy glanced toward the door and lowered his voice to a hoarse whisper. "The big deal is that the party guy owes me fifteen hundred bucks, and I need it right now." He grabbed Jimmy by the front of his sweatshirt and tugged him a step closer. "Bill Rohrbaugh assigns the insurance contracts at Continental Container, and I can't let him leave town thinking I'm too broke to cover my gambling debts. That's a bad image for business."

"You mean you bet against your own partner?"

Teddy released his grip on the sweatshirt and frowned. "There's no such thing as partners," he said. "Now are you gonna drive us up there, or not?"

The trip took longer than Teddy said it would. He claimed he'd been to the cabin twice before, but never at night, and now, cruising the pitch-black mountain roads, he had trouble recognizing landmarks. Jimmy was reasonably familiar with the area—he'd attended church camp in these woods one summer when he was twelve, right after his mother died —but none of the roads or driveway entrances were marked with anything more revealing than occasional blue or red reflector discs, so he had to rely on Teddy's sense of direction. At each trail that split from the main road, Teddy leaned out his window to scrutinize the invisible landscape, claimed a flicker of recognition, then reversed himself and told Jimmy to drive on.

After half a dozen of these false alarms, Teddy suddenly said, "Stop here," with an urgency that made Jimmy think they'd found the spot at last. But then Teddy stuck his head out into the cool night air and vomited down the side of the Bronco. Jimmy figured that would probably bring the evening to a close, but Mr. Rohrbaugh had apparently nodded off at some point along the way and had no complaints about the change in Teddy's condition.

"I get carsick when I ride in back," Teddy explained, then stumbled from the car into the edge of the dark woods.

"I think we've got a couple of drunks on our hands," Willa said, though she didn't seem upset. Jimmy listened to the soft snoring of Mr. Rohrbaugh in the back seat.

"I thought your father was pretty sober," Jimmy whispered.

"If he were sober we wouldn't be here. But people kept buying him drinks all night because he won the tournament."

"He sure holds it well."

"Only up to a point," she said. "Then he goes down like he got hit with a tranquilizer dart."

"That's not a bad way to be," he said, thinking of the times his own father had drunk too much in public. Willa seemed genuinely at ease with her father's present state, even amused by it, and that was an attitude he simply couldn't fathom. Maybe it meant she had the warmest heart he'd ever come across; or maybe it meant she had no heart at all.

Teddy lunged from the black weeds back to the side of the Bronco and leaned his head through the rear window. "We're there," he said. "I can hear the music."

Jimmy turned off the motor and listened. The faint strains of an electric guitar filtered up through the woods on their right. Or maybe it wasn't an electric guitar. The notes were so muffled and fragmented they might have come from any number of instruments—saxophones, fiddles, a synthesizer, even an accordion. It was music reduced to its most general form, a charming seepage of sounds with no melody, no rhythm, nothing but the loose wash of an undefined harmony weaving up through the trees. "I think it's coming from down there," he said, pointing into the darkness on Willa's side of the Bronco. "But it still sounds pretty far away."

"I remember now," said Teddy, climbing back inside. "That's the turnoff." He pointed to a pair of red reflectors glowing by the side of the road forty yards ahead.

Jimmy started the engine and eased the Bronco forward. "You still want to do this?" he asked Willa. "I mean, with your father asleep and all—"

"Hell, yes," she said brightly. "This is the most fun I've had all weekend."

Jimmy steered between the reflectors and nudged the Bronco over the packed arch of the shoulder. "I can't see what the driveway's like in front of us," he said. "The headlights are angled too high."

"Well, it's not actually a driveway," Teddy said. "It's sort of a trail the guy scraped out with a backhoe. So take it easy going down."

Jimmy rode the brake hard as the Bronco groaned along the steep slope. Teddy had been right about the ruts, which were deep enough to scrape the front axle, but gravity and momentum kept the tires from miring in the mud.

"We'll never get back up this hill," said Willa.

"No need to," Teddy told her. "This lane runs all the way through the property. It comes out on one of the county roads farther down the mountain."

Jimmy kept his eyes on the narrow cut of trees ahead of them, and wound the Bronco slowly down the switchback trail. After a few minutes the music grew more distinct, rising now above the noise of their engine, and Jimmy caught glimpses of lights flickering through the overgrown woods.

Willa suddenly put a hand on his shoulder. "Stop," she said. Jimmy jammed the brake and the Bronco skidded gently to a halt. "Look over there," she said, pointing into the trees on her side of the cut. Teddy leaned forward between the seats, and the three of them stared out at the tangle of undergrowth. Twenty yards ahead, just inside the angle of the headlight beams, a cluster of tiny red lights glowed in the shadows.

"Those are eyes," said Teddy.

"A family of possum, most likely," Jimmy said. "Or maybe raccoons."

"Why are they all staring at us?" Willa asked. "Why don't they run away or hide or something?"

"We're too scary to run from," Jimmy told her. "Instinct makes them keep an eye on whatever they think might be dangerous."

"He's right," said Teddy. "Watch this." He reached across to the steering wheel and honked the horn. None of the eyes moved. "I used to go night-hunting this way," he went on. "What you do is go out into a clearing and lean on the horn a few times, then shine a light up into the trees. Whatever's up there'll be watching you, and the light reflects in their eyes. They won't even blink if they can help it. Then you just draw a bead and pop 'em right between the glow spots."

Jimmy eased off the brake and let the Bronco roll forward. The family of eyes receded into the darkness. "It's illegal to hunt that way," he pointed out.

"True enough," said Teddy. "But it sure saves a lot of time and legwork."

"I know something about raccoons," Willa said. "When a baby raccoon cries, it sounds just like a human baby."

Teddy snorted and leaned further forward. "I guess you picked that up at college."

Willa crossed her arms and stared straight ahead into the flurry of moths batting through the high beams. "I'll tell you what I picked up at college: not a goddamn thing."

Teddy took a small tube of breath spray from his inside suit pocket and squirted a long stream into his mouth. "Well, I'll tell you what a baby raccoon sounds like, because I know. It sounds like a goddamn baby raccoon."

Teddy's equilibrium was returning, but so was his native belligerence, and Jimmy began to scan the woods ahead for some timely distraction. "I think I see the band lights," he said, and it was true: as they rounded the final bend of the grade, the dense trees parted to a broad clearing. Forty yards to their left was the cabin, and beside it the elevated platform where the band, in a flood of colored lights, was now blasting its way through a frenzied version of an old Rolling Stones song. A hundred people, maybe more, danced wildly on a rocky patch of ground before the bandstand, some of the men without their shirts, and nearly everyone with large plastic drinking cups in their hands. Of those who weren't dancing, most clustered in smaller groups across the hillside, a few here by a fallen tree trunk, a few there on the cabin porch, some weaving in the shadows behind the makeshift stage. A stream of solitary drunks stumbled in and out of the woods, hitching up their pants and waving to their friends, searching, most likely, for bathrooms or beer. At least a dozen lay passed out or sleeping on a gallery of rough blankets spread against one bank of the clearing, their arms and legs splayed in every direction. Pickup trucks and ATVs littered the low end of the clearing, all crowded haphazardly along the side of the grade like shells in a junkyard. But the raw edge of the music carved its own electric space up through the tall cathedral of trees, and for a moment Jimmy felt overwhelmed by the spectacle. That so much color and sound and human celebration could take place in the middle of a darkened mountain forest seemed nothing short of miraculous. But at the same time he felt timid in the face of it all, an alien in an indecipherable landscape. How could people dance so hard where none of the ground was level?

"My God," said Willa. "I think we just found out what happened to the Druids."

Teddy laughed and swung open the car door. "Park it anywhere," he said. "And if Bill wakes up, tell him to look for me at the cabin." He got out and started across the field, his white suit glowing in the headlights.

"If my dad wakes up, he'll probably make us leave. I don't think this is the kind of party he was expecting." She pulled her new sweater down low over the front of her dress. "I wish I'd worn jeans. I look like somebody's fairy god-mother."

"I've got a sweat suit in the back," Jimmy told her. "You can wear that if you want."

"Great," she said.

Jimmy pulled the Bronco onto a firm stretch of shoulder and parked it. "It's in my golf bag," he said. "I'll go dig it out."

He circled to the rear hatch and rummaged for the clothes. "I don't have any shoes for you," he said.

"I'll go barefoot."

He took out the rolled-up sweats and sniffed them. He'd worn them the day before to clean out a poison ivy patch between the fourth and fifth fairways, but they didn't seem too rank. He closed the hatch and climbed back into the Bronco. He'd already shut the door behind him before he realized Willa had taken off both her sweater and her dress and was sitting beside him now in nothing but her under-pants and bra. At first he thought he should jump back out and apologize like some dumb kid, but that would have been too phony to stomach. His shyness had dried up long ago, and it took more than the sight of a little bare skin to sweep him into panic. He turned toward her on the seat and handed over the sweat suit as casually as if he were selling golf tees. For her part, Willa didn't seem embarrassed at all, but Jimmy still felt uneasy. He couldn't tell if he was being brazenly rude or infinitely polite.

"Can you imagine if my dad woke up right now?" she said, and Jimmy felt a shiver run through him. But Mr. Rohrbaugh was still slumped peacefully against the door-frame, rattling out his deep, slow breaths. Willa quickly slipped the sweatshirt over her head and shook out the bottoms by the waistband. "Which is crazy, really," she went on, shoving her feet awkwardly down the pant legs. "I mean, he wouldn't think twice if I was sitting here in a bikini. Why do you suppose that is?"

"It's just part of the rule book," Jimmy said. "Some things are out of bounds."

"You're cute," she said, and got out of the Bronco.

Jimmy followed her across the clearing to the fringes of the dance crowd. The band had now launched into a bone-jarring attack on a recent top-forty tune he'd once liked but had finally grown sick of. The sound of it moved right through him, tangible and rude, like a current too strong to resist. Still, it was an opportunity, so he touched Willa's arm to ask her to dance. She smiled sourly and shook her head, then circled slowly away from him toward the side of the stage. Jimmy trailed after her, though he wondered if maybe she wanted him to get lost.

When she reached the corner of the risers, Willa put her hands over her ears and stepped directly in front of the am-plifier. Then she turned toward him, letting the volume pound against her back. She called out something to him, but it was lost in the thunder of the music.

The band was better than he remembered. The guy on keyboards had apparently learned how to hook up his equipment without blowing a speaker, and he played now in a cool balance between abandon and control. The vocalist was new, a redhead, and Jimmy could see from the cut of her gown that the band was tinkering with its image, moving away from country-western into something more soulful, a little closer to mainstream, maybe, but still played as if each wailing note might be its last.

As he moved in closer Willa stepped away from the amp and they walked together toward the back edge of the clearing, where an enormous fallen tree sloped upward into the darkness.

"It was like taking a shower," she said happily.

"What was?"

"Standing in front of the speaker like that. I could really feel it." She glanced at him sideways. "Better than cocaine," she said.

"I wouldn't know."

She sat back against the ragged trunk. "Well, I would. That's why I'm in the market for a new college."

"You got kicked out for doing drugs?"

"I got hospitalized for doing drugs. Now my dad figures I need a different environment."

"What happened?"

"Nothing very dramatic. I mean, I wasn't trying to kill myself or anything, I just screwed up. Big weekend, lots of parties—I drank too much beer one night and then hooked up with a couple of friends who had some better coke than I was used to. For a while I really thought I was gonna die."

"Sounds pretty scary."

"Yeah, it was. I never passed out, I just kept getting colder and colder. It was like I could feel my whole body shutting down, piece by piece, and there was no way to stop it. I had to concentrate as hard as I could just to keep breathing. But I knew if I could ride it out long enough I'd be okay." She smiled at him and spread her palms. "And here I am, back on the old dance floor. No particular damage."

"I'm glad," he said lamely.

The drummer broke into a staccato burst that punctuated the end of their song, and the redheaded singer mumbled into the microphone that the Radio Actives were through for the night. A chorus of protests rose from the dance crowd, but the musicians had already begun to disconnect their equipment, oblivious, it seemed, to their own popularity.

Willa swung a leg up and straddled the tree trunk. "Your turn," she said. "Tell me something true."

"No lobster ever makes it out of Iowa alive."

Willa shook her head and pulled a brittle strip of bark from the tree. "You're a disappointment," she said. She climbed carefully to her feet and began to walk away from him along the angle of the trunk.

"I wouldn't go barefoot on this tree if I were you," he said. "We get a lot of black widows in these parts."

She stopped about ten steps up the angle and casually began to scan the bark around her feet. "I'm not too concerned. Statistics are on my side." She smiled down at him and started to say something more, but the look on her face suddenly darkened, and for a second Jimmy thought she'd actually been bitten.

"What's the matter?" he asked.

Willa descended the trunk and stepped gingerly into the dirt beside him. "Trouble in paradise," she said, staring past him toward the cabin. He turned in time to see Mumford sailing like a half-folded sheet from the elevated porch, clearing the steps altogether and landing hard on his side in the rocky yard. "Ouch," said Willa, but there was something like a laugh in her voice, and Jimmy began to realize how tough she really was.

He took her hand and they started together toward Mumford, who rolled onto his back and slowly pushed himself up by his elbows. A shirtless man in bluejeans and work boots stepped to the edge of the porch and folded his arms across his sunburned chest. He wasn't big, but he was muscular, with a loose, hardened look about him, as if he worked on road crews, maybe, or in rock quarries, running heavy equipment.

The fight, if that's what it had been, was apparently over,

since Mumford seemed in no particular hurry to pick himself up from the dirt. Even so, Jimmy knew better than to barge too clumsily into the aftermath.

"Hi, Teddy," he said as he and Willa made their way up beside him in the yard. "How's it going?" The man on the porch glanced briefly at Jimmy, sizing him up and dismissing him in a single flick of the eye. Then he turned his glare back on Mumford, who ran his fingers nonchalantly through his hair and squinted over his shoulder toward the band.

"At the moment," he said, "I have no opinion."

The man on the porch walked heavily down the steps. "Don't expect to get your hardware back," he said, pointing a thick finger at Mumford's face. "And don't you ever pull a stunt like that around me again." Then he climbed back up the steps, taking them two at a time, and disappeared into the cabin.

"Looks like you took a bad spill," Jimmy said as he helped Mumford to his feet.

"Yeah. It's a good thing I'm drunk, or I mighta got hurt," he said, smiling and straightening his tie. He brushed clumsily at the dirt caked on the right side of his pants, then wiped a trickle of blood from his nose onto his coat sleeve. "I'll probably have to get this dry-cleaned," he said, fingering a tear in the breast pocket.

"What was that all about?" Willa asked. "Who was that guy?"

Mumford shrugged. "Just some guy." Then he looked

around slowly, scrutinizing the trees. "You know, I don't think this is the right party, after all."

The three of them walked together across the noisy clearing, weaving their way through scores of drunken lovers, stopping periodically for Mumford to tilt his head back in an effort to stanch his nosebleed. As they neared the Bronco, Mumford lurched ahead and peered in the window at Willa's father, who was still sleeping comfortably in the back seat. Jimmy put a hand on Mumford's shoulder to guide him clear of the door, but Mumford shook it off and stumbled toward the rear of the Bronco. "You kids go back to the party," he said, sitting awkwardly on the corner of the bumper. "I'm still a little woozy from that fall. If it's all the same to you, I'm not quite up to a buggy ride just yet." He closed his eyes and leaned slowly forward, cupping his head in his hands. "Just give me twenty minutes, I'll be fine."

Jimmy turned to Willa, but she was already walking away. He followed her down past the bandstand to the edge of the trees and caught up with her at the fallen trunk.

"I don't know what to say," he told her.

She nodded. "A lot goes on." Then she surprised him with a smile. "You're a golfer, right? Say something about that. Tell me your most glorious golf story."

A tiredness fell across him like a wave, and he sat back against the rough slope of the trunk. "I don't have one," he told her.

"Oh, come on. All golfers have golf stories. My father's

no good at all, but even he comes home every week with some golf miracle he's just dying to talk about. Did you ever win any big tournaments?"

"No," he said, and for the first time it came to him that he probably never would.

"Ever come close?"

"Once, I guess. Three years ago in the state juniors championship. I blew a three-stroke lead on the final hole."

"Did you come in second?"

"I didn't come in at all. I was disqualified."

"What was it—did they catch you cheating?"

Jimmy laughed. "No, nothing like that. It was stupid. I got into a fistfight with my caddy and never finished the round."

Willa sat beside him on the trunk. "Why'd you do that?"

Jimmy shrugged. "He handed me the wrong club. I guess I got mad."

Willa giggled and took him by the arm. "You're a dangerous character," she said.

He decided to let it go at that. There was no sense dragging up any more of the story than he had to—no need to tell her that the caddy was his father, or that his father was a violent alcoholic who had drunk himself nearly into a stupor by the eighteenth hole. Willa's father was harmless—a gentle, snoring businessman who'd had a few too many; she might not understand the sort of timber rattler other drunks could be.

Teddy Mumford was a rattler-in-the-making. He'd pushed his luck tonight, and that had clearly caused him some damage—but he probably hadn't learned anything. Mumford was a guy with a wrong attitude, and even if it didn't get him killed tonight, it surely would someday.

But he knew Willa was right—in his own way, he was every bit as dangerous a character as Teddy Mumford. True, he didn't drink or smoke or gamble or do drugs, but that didn't mean much: there were far more serious dependencies to wrestle with. Even now, there was a ticking in his chest he couldn't answer.

"This is nice," he said quietly, and Willa leaned her head against his shoulder. They sat for a long moment staring into the black curtain of the woods, propping each other up.

Behind them, the band continued packing up its gear, and he heard someone offer five hundred dollars if they'd stay for another set. "We've got people waiting at home," was the only reply.

Jimmy thought of the graffiti he'd scrubbed this morning from the bathroom stalls in the men's locker room. Most of it had been the same standard, ugly stuff he'd seen in public rest rooms everywhere—in high schools, bus depots, and restaurants: nothing clean and nothing memorable. But today he'd found one happy declaration scratched into the paint of the lavatory door: *I kissed a girl,* it read.

I kissed a girl.

The pathetic innocence of that line amazed him. *I kissed a girl,* as if some poor kid's life had suddenly become everything he had dreamed of. *I kissed a girl,* as if something that small were all it took. Such unschooled hope was downright staggering; and remembering it now, even with Willa pressing a soft cheek against his sleeve, he had to think hard not to cry.

‹ ‹ ‹

Survivalists

Rod rushed through the dark cabin to the kitchen, the wet sack in front of him, trying not to drip on the fake-oriental rugs. Fins poked precariously through the bag in several places, and he worried that the soggy bottom might not survive even this short trip in from the car. He moved smoothly through the musty rooms, his arms locked beneath the weight of the catch. When at last he eased the sack onto the porcelain drain beside the sink, he felt a wave of relief.

Rod hadn't cleaned fish in years, and he wasn't sure he still remembered how. In any case, he was glad Brenda wasn't here to watch him, to look over his shoulder while he tried to reacquaint himself with the old techniques. One thing he had discovered in these last few weeks was that he

couldn't work with her around. She had a more critical eye than anyone he'd ever known. Sometimes, when she bore down on him with her full concentration, he felt as if she were performing an autopsy on his every move.

He didn't really blame her. The spontaneity that had launched them into marriage had proved difficult to maintain, and already he'd sensed that the sober, daylight hours might be their downfall. That was why he'd rented such a secluded cabin—so they'd be forced to get to know each other better. In a way, the plan had already worked. He knew now that she hated cabins.

She had agreed to drive down to the lake with him today only to avoid being left alone in the place, cooped up with no television or stereo. Rod had hoped that once he got her to the water she might feel more enthusiastic. But she never did.

He moved to the dark wall by the kitchen doorway and found the light switch with his elbow. His hands were filthy and covered with the stink that always accompanied fishing —though he'd never figured out whether the smell came from the fish or the worms. That afternoon at least a dozen worms had burst in his grasp as he tried to hold their wriggling bodies still enough to thread the curve of the hook through their full length. And of the fish he'd caught that day—of the fish he and Brenda had caught that day—all but one had swallowed the hook, forcing him to pry their mouths apart and tear loose the tender workings of their throats.

Retrieving a swallowed hook was certainly worse than baiting one, but in fact Rod hated to do either one. He was embarrassed with himself for feeling so squeamish, but he couldn't help it. He had confessed this to Brenda while he was baiting her hook, and regretted it at once.

"I wish you'd grow up," she told him. "It's natural to kill things. That's how we survive."

Rod thought it over. Maybe she was right. After all, fish were certainly no high point of Creation. They didn't even have enough evolutionary development to close their eyes. And worms weren't much of anything—just rich pieces of dirt. Maybe guilt was not a proper consideration here.

He had still been weighing the pros and cons when the catfish struck his line. He raised it instantly from the murky water and swung it high up the grassy bank. Then as quickly as he could—quickly, to keep it from flopping back down to the lake—he pinned it with his foot and maneuvered his hands around the sleek, fat body, carefully avoiding the stinging fins. It was a beautiful catch, over eighteen inches long, and Rod realized immediately that he'd landed it only by the sheerest luck. The hook was hardly in the fish at all. It dangled, blue and gleaming, from the lower lip, a slight snag only. Rod knew that if he hadn't pulled this catfish up so swiftly, robbing it of its own reaction time, it could easily have slipped his line with almost no harm done. This fish had not been caught by skill; it had simply run afoul of a blind reflex quicker than its own.

A sudden movement in the paper sack startled Rod into a backward spin from the sink. He stumbled against the gas heater by the wall.

"Jesus," he said, steadying himself against the countertop. He hadn't expected any of the fish to be still alive. They'd all been out of the water for—how long? He'd left the lake a half hour ago at least. Then there was the time it took him to disassemble the poles and put away the tackle; and before that, in the space between the catfish and the dark, the time that he and Brenda had argued, disagreeing about dinner. So these fish had been high and dry for well over an hour, some even longer. He didn't know what the biological facts were in a case like this, but he'd always assumed that fish didn't get along on land any better than people did underwater. Apparently he was wrong.

He dumped the bag into the sink and looked carefully at the assortment of fish. None of them seemed to have any flop left in them now. They all looked dead. But that's the way it was with fish—even when they were still spasming on the lake bank and pumping their gills, they already looked dead. It was the only look they knew. Rod blamed it on their eyes.

He turned the cold-water tap on full and let the stream splash down hard into the jumble of fish, thinking this might wash away some of the grass and dirt they'd picked up from the lake bank. He somehow thought they should be made clean and neat before he gutted them. What he hadn't expected was that some of the fish would be revived by the sudden blast of water. But now he counted five fish still moving their gills, straining for whatever refreshment the water might give. One of the two small bass was still alive, as were three brim. The catfish was still heaving, in and out, like a small lung living on its own. All the sunnies were dead.

Rod took out an old spoon from the drawer beneath the dish rack and eased his hand down over the head of the first sunny, folding the sharp fins against the stiffening body. He had already been jabbed once by this same fish when he had tried to extract the hook from its mouth, and he wasn't about to get careless now—even a dead fish could do damage.

He could tell it was the same fish that cut him by the way he'd broken its jaw going after the hook. He'd more or less unhinged it, and it now hung very low and crooked from the fish's face. The disfiguration gave the sunny a different kind of look. It not only looked dead, it looked surprised.

Rod gripped the tail tightly with his fingertips and began to rake the spoon harshly across the side of the fish, stripping off scales. They flaked away easily, and in less than a minute he'd cleaned all the way down to the smooth silvery-yellow skin.

Next, he slipped the edge of the spoon under the bony

fins jutting from the fish's sides, and with two quick motions toward the head, snapped the sharp bones off into the sink. To remove the dorsal fin, he made a cut with a paring knife across the ridge of the back, just below the base of the fin, and pulled it forward toward the head. It peeled away easily.

So far everything was going as smoothly as he could have hoped for, and he began to wish, in spite of himself, that Brenda were here to witness his success. She would never have believed him capable.

"You'd never make it in the wilderness," she had told him, laughing at the fuss he made when the hook caught in his thumb.

"I could do all right," he said, trying to suppress his indignation. He swished his fingers through the water to wash away the blood.

"I'm sure every man likes to think that. But not many could." She began to wave her pole slowly back and forth, drawing her float in a meandering zigzag across the shallows.

"There's no bait on that," he said, pointing out toward her line.

"I know. I'm trying it the hard way." She fished in silence while he rummaged through the tackle box for a Band-Aid. "What would you do if there was a war?" she asked suddenly.

"What do you mean?" He gave up on the Band-Aid and picked up his pole again.

"If there was a war—a nuclear war—and our whole society collapsed, what would you do to survive?"

"I don't think it'll ever come to that."

She slapped the frail tip of her pole against the surface of the lake. "Which means if it ever does come to that, you won't know what to do." She touched the tip of her pole to the water again, this time so gently it barely made a ripple. "Randy's got it all worked out."

"I'm sure."

"He does—I've seen his stash. He's got guns and jugged water and about a ton of canned food up at his Uncle Billy's place on South Mountain. The band played a gig there a couple of weeks ago."

"Sounds to me like Uncle Billy's the one who's got it all worked out."

"Billy's in jail now. That's what the party was for— Randy wanted to give him a big send-off." She shook her head. "Randy could be real sweet sometimes."

Rod pulled up his line to check his bait. Small fish had been picking at his hook, and he had only half a worm left.

"It was a real blowout party," she went on. "They set us up on this outdoor stage in front of Billy's house and we cranked up our amps as high as they'd go. They probably heard us in the next county. It was great."

While Rod loaded up his hook with part of another worm, he tried to imagine an answer to his wife's question.

Maybe this was exactly what he needed from her—reminders that he hadn't put much thought into basic survival.

"I'd go to the library," he said finally. She turned to him and frowned. "I'd take out books on carpentry, and mechanics, farming, and whatever else looked like it might help us get along. With a knapsack full of the right books, I could probably survive anywhere, indefinitely." He was pleased with his reasoning, but Brenda remained unimpressed. She tossed a pebble into the water by his float.

"And while you're checking out library books, everybody else will be getting guns and knives. You wouldn't stand a chance." She shook her head, but smiled, as if he were a lost cause she couldn't quite abandon. "Survival isn't something you can look up in the reference section."

The sunny was ready now, either for gutting or for having its head removed. He couldn't remember which was supposed to come first, or even if it mattered. He opted for decapitation, and sawed efficiently through the fish just behind the gills. After that it was easy to slit the underside and scrape the organs out into the sink.

He held the fish open before him like a book and thought about the bones. They seemed thoroughly enmeshed in the soft white meat, and he wasn't sure how to go about stripping them away without tearing up the remainder of the fish. He tried pulling at the spine, but that didn't work at all: the fish seemed to disintegrate in his hands. By the time he'd picked away all the tiny ribs, only two bite-sized pieces remained. He held the tiny fillets in his palms and considered them. Not much to show for his efforts. But if he could salvage at least this much meat from each of these dozen fish, that would be enough for a meal for the two of them. Brenda wouldn't eat much anyway—if she ate any of it at all. She was probably filling up right now on steak and quail.

The catfish began to crawl around over the other fish. Rod hated to see this. All he wanted was for them to die peacefully in their oxygen-starved comas. He didn't want to have to force matters.

Damned catfish. Rod remembered a news story he'd seen about walking catfish. Someplace down in Florida people kept finding catfish in their yards. The fish were just passing through, looking for more hospitable waters. Their old haunts had been polluted by a chemical spill, so they had taken to the land, dragging themselves hundreds of yards, using their front fins like little crutches.

This catfish might take a very long time to die.

When he had gone fishing as a boy, his grandmother had never let him keep a catfish. "Too much trouble to clean," she always said. Catfish didn't have scales; they had to be skinned.

"I'll skin it," he always volunteered.

"I'd have to show you how, and I just don't want to mess with it. Anytime you hook a catfish, just throw him right back in."

That was always the rule. No turtles, no brim smaller than

his hand, and no catfish whatsoever. Now that he'd actually brought one back for cleaning, he had no idea how to begin.

He set the catfish aside and continued working on the other fish. When he came to the first largemouth bass, he thought again of Brenda. This was the first fish she had caught—and after she'd swung it from the water to the lake bank, she insisted that he be the one to remove it from her line. He grumbled, but set about doing it. Then just as he finally dislodged the hook from the fish's throat, she swatted at a bee with her pole. He saw it coming, even had his mouth open to tell her not to move, but it was too late. The hook was deep in his thumb before he could utter a sound.

He looked closely now at his damaged thumb. It was turning a bluish white around the snag. He turned the tap on full again, thinking he should try to clean the wound before working on any more fish, and stuck his thumb under the stream. He wondered when he had had his last tetanus shot, or even if a tetanus shot would help. He thought about particles of worm in his blood.

He didn't mind the pain of the water slicing into his cut. Pain that came with a cleansing was good pain. He was convinced that treating injuries too gently only prolonged the agony.

The wound looked pretty clean, but the stink was still there. He squeezed some dishwashing liquid onto his fingers to cover up the odor. After he rinsed this off, his hands smelled even worse—still fishy-wormy, but now slightly sweet.

The catfish moved again, revived by the running water. Rod quickly shut off the tap. The last thing he wanted was to keep this fish alive. He had to admit, though, it was quite a catfish. Even the dove hunters had admired it.

They'd heard him yelling when Brenda jerked the hook through his thumb, and came down from the woods to see what the trouble was. Brenda had been uneasy when she first saw the group approaching—three men with rifles cradled in their arms.

"Relax," he told her. He knew there was nothing to worry about: the social order hadn't collapsed yet. Besides, he recognized Ed Betzger. Ed was the one who'd first told him about this place, and had even arranged the cabin rental for him.

"Hey, you two," Ed called. "How's it going?"

"Pretty good, I guess," Rod answered, trudging up the slope to meet him. The two of them shook hands, and then Ed gestured expansively to his companions.

"Rod, this is my brother Lewis," he said, "and my brother-in-law Bobby." Bobby, in the background, nodded hello across Ed's shoulder. Lewis shifted his shotgun to the crook of his left arm and extended his hand. "How're ya doing?" he said. He was a short, round-faced man, slightly puffier than his brother but just as amiable-looking.

"Rod here used to be the pro golfer out at the Country Club," Ed told them.

Lewis smiled. "I don't think I ever met a pro golfer before. That must be quite the life."

"Well, it keeps me outside a lot," Rod said. "That's always good."

"I meant the money part, playing in all those million-dollar tournaments," said Lewis. "Who gives a shit about being outside? Hell, I hate working outside. Put a roof over my head any day."

"Lewis drives a backhoe for the county," Ed explained.

"It's always too hot," Lewis went on, "or else it's too cold or too wet or some damn thing."

"That don't seem to keep you home when dove season rolls around," said Bobby, clapping a hand on Lewis' back.

"That's different," Lewis said. "That's by choice."

"I was out at the golf course the other day," Ed said to Rod. "Had to flush some lime deposits from the shower heads in the women's locker room. Jimmy and Bev said to tell you hello if I saw you. They knew I'd be heading up this way."

"Thanks."

"They think you got a pretty raw deal. A lot of people do. Shirley Stonesifer got up a petition to make the Board hire you back."

"Who's Shirley Stonesifer?"

"You know—Shirley Davies. She left her husband and

took her old name back." He grinned. "Her and me are kinda seeing each other now."

Ed Betzger and Shirley Davies? Of all the news he'd heard lately, this was the most bizarre.

"Well, that's nice of Shirley," Rod said. "But really, there were plenty of good reasons for the Board to fire me. I was pretty lousy at running the pro shop. Shirley ought to know that as well as anybody. Hell, I lost her seven iron."

"No, she got that back," said Ed, raising his eyebrows in amazement. "It was the damnedest thing. She went down to her husband's real estate office to make him sign some papers, and there was a guy there, some client looking to buy a house, and this guy had Shirley's seven iron with him. He had a bum leg and he was using it for a cane. Said he found it in a parking lot someplace. She bought it off him for ten bucks."

Rod didn't know what to say.

"Anyway," Ed went on, "it wouldn't surprise me if the Board asked you to come back. From what I hear, a lot of the members are pretty fed up with the way Glen Hanshaw runs things. They all think he's crazy as a goddamn loon."

Rod smiled. "He may be, but I don't blame him for firing me. I was lousy at running the pro shop. Never could make myself do the paperwork."

"You shouldn'ta had to," Ed said. "They shoulda hired a general manager for that stuff. They still might, if they can get Glen Hanshaw out of the way."

"I guess Teddy Mumford's leading the mutiny."

Ed spat into the tall grass. "That shithead couldn't lead water downhill. He still owes me the insurance money for that air conditioner Hal Sykes won off me in the Member-Guest tournament. I don't think the bastard even sent in the claim."

"Well, keep after him."

"You can bet on it." Ed shaded his eyes with his hand and squinted down at Brenda, who was standing on the bank, arms folded, watching them. "I'm surprised to see you newlyweds outside the cabin. If I'd known you were looking for something to do, I'd have asked you to come dove hunting with us."

Rod nodded toward a bulging burlap sack dangling from Lewis' shoulder. "Looks like you guys did all right on your own."

"Well," said Lewis, "first day of the season is always good." He pointed to the pile of fish at Brenda's feet. "Seems you've had some luck yourself. That catfish is a beauty."

"We've got plenty if you'd like to take some along," Rod offered. Ed smiled.

"No, thanks, we've got steaks waiting for us up at Bobby's place." He turned and pointed up the slope through the trees. "It's about a quarter mile over that way. How about you two joining us? We've sure got more birds than we'll know what to do with. And you can't beat a steak-and-dove combination. We might even scrounge up some quail."

"That's nice of you, Ed, but I guess we'll just stick with our fish."

Ed shrugged. "Well, suit yourself."

Rod felt the urge to explain further, but there was nothing to say.

After Ed and his clan had climbed back up the hillside through the trees, Rod unscrewed the three sections of his bamboo pole and emptied the bait carton onto the bank. A few startled worms tumbled into the water.

"Giving up?" Brenda asked, nudging the overturned carton with her toe.

"I guess we've caught enough."

"Suits me." She dropped her own pole onto the grass beside him. "I heard what that Ed guy said about your job. It'd be great if they took you back."

Rod began to wind his line carefully around the top section of bamboo. "I might not want to go back," he said, not looking at her. "I might want to give the tour another try."

He heard her sigh. "Everybody's got choices to make," she said.

"What's that supposed to mean?"

"Well, one thing it means is maybe you should've said we'd have dinner with those guys. You can't make a smart decision if you don't know what's going on."

Rod tucked the barb of the hook into the clip of the plastic float, then set to work on Brenda's pole, winding her line tightly around the frail bamboo. "You go ahead if you want to," he told her. "Have yourself some steak."

"Well, I know I don't want to eat these fish," she said. They were quiet for a long time after that, and Rod wondered if that meant they'd reached some kind of decision.

"What about you?" he asked, breaking the silence. "What would you do if there was a nuclear war?"

She stared out across the lake. "Whatever I had to, I suppose."

"But I mean would you stay with me?"

Brenda smiled and brushed her hair back from her face. "Only if you change your game plan."

He thought about that as he put the fish and tackle into the back of the car. Change his game plan, just like that. Change it, and everything would work out fine. But what did that mean? Change it to what? What the hell did she expect him to do? Join the army? Buy guns with his unemployment checks? Okay, so the tour idea was a long shot. An expensive long shot. But what else did he have? He wasn't cut out to be a Club pro, he knew that. The busywork drove him nuts—order this, reorder that, keep track of the accounts, keep track of the inventory. Keep track of the gossip, keep track of the feuds. He hated it.

So what was left? Selling buckets of balls at the driving range? Handing out free games at the putt-putt? It had to be the tour—there was no other choice. So why wasn't she with him in this? The more he thought about it, the madder he got.

And he was still thinking about it when he got in the car and drove away, leaving her to figure things out on her own.

Now he thought about it again as he stood poised over the sink, knife in hand, waiting for the catfish to die. He was infinitely calmer now, and as he stared down at the sink full of fish parts, his confusion began suddenly to lift.

It was hard to know what people really wanted. For a long time he'd been foggy even about what he wanted for himself. Seven years ago he thought he wanted to marry his college sweetheart, so he married her. Five years ago he thought he wanted to go on the PGA tour, so he hit the road. Both had been bad choices.

Now he was married again, this time to a relative stranger. He knew she didn't trust him, not at all—and why should she? He was a jerk, a guy who could leave a woman stranded at a lake on her honeymoon.

But still she had let herself get caught up by him, had married him, as he had married her, on gut feeling alone, with no time to think, no tangible reason to believe it might work, no logical odds in their favor beyond the pure luck of the draw. But they'd been right, he knew it. Reckless and irrational, but ultimately right. He couldn't begin to explain it, but there it was.

The tour idea was stupid. How the hell could he expect

to make a comeback? The body fails, bit by bit; his peak had come and gone. No matter how much he worked on his game, he'd never be as good as he was five years ago—and he hadn't been good enough even then.

But marriage didn't have to be that way. Age could be a definite advantage—things could be learned, mistakes didn't have to be repeated. Looking at it that way, a second shot might even stand a better chance than the first. Especially if he paid attention to the hazards.

He'd take back the Country Club job if they offered it. Or he'd sign on at the driving range. Or he'd man the counter at the putt-putt. Or he'd sell encyclopedias door to door. He'd do anything he had to.

The catfish crawled against the side of the sink, looking for some way out. For a long time Rod watched it scratching at the porcelain, watched the gray gills pulsing in and out. At last he took a washtub from beneath the sink and filled it, then picked up the big fish in both hands and slid it gently down into the fresh water.

He carried the washtub very carefully to the car, not spilling a drop.